The Keepinnit Reels 2: Acoustic Boogaloo

Michael Pollick

Published by Michael Pollick, 2024.

This is a work of fiction. Similarities to real people, places, or events are entirely coincidental.

THE KEEPINNIT REELS 2: ACOUSTIC BOOGALOO

First edition. July 22, 2024.

ISBN: 979-8227910042

Written by Michael Pollick.

Also by Michael Pollick

Michael Pollick's Proving Ground
Michael Pollick's Proving Ground
The Keepinnit Reels
The Keepinnit Reels 2: Acoustic Boogaloo

Table of Contents

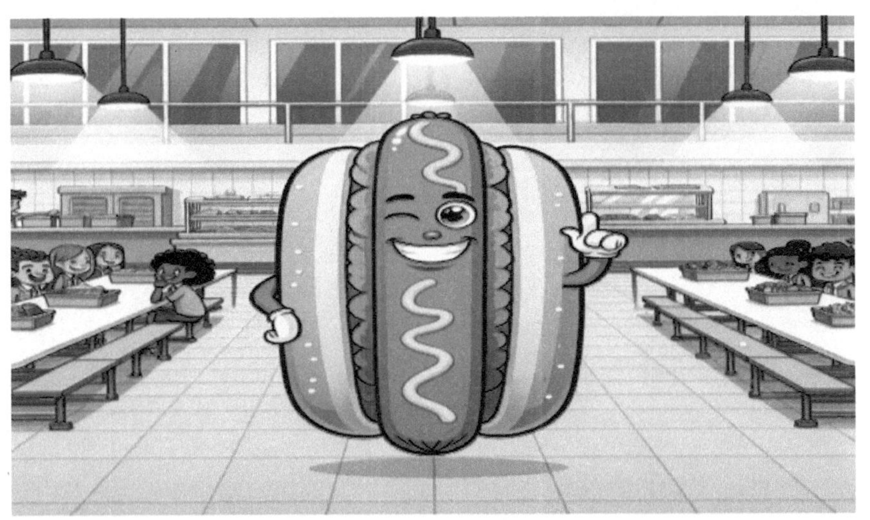

When The Wiener Winked: Cafeteria Food Sponsored By Big Pharma

School cafeteria food has become the low-hanging fruit Jello of the humor essay community, but it got there honestly. My elementary school handed out a lunch menu every Monday morning, so customers could decide whether to pack a lunch or cough up the 35 cents. Hamburgers and pizza automatically got a free pass, while dubious choices like beans and weenies or grilled cheese and tomato soup usually got a hard "no" from me.

There was one item on the menu, however, that put the fear of Pepto Bismol in me. It sounded innocent enough on paper. A slice of white bread, barely toasted, a government-grade hotdog, and a thin slice of American cheese. Ladies and gentlemen of the culinary jury, I give you: The Wiener Wink. To this day, I have no idea where the name came from, but I suspect the "wink" was an inside joke at headquarters.

Wiener winks were served without a single condiment. No ketchup, mustard, onions, or relish. I believe they also ran it through the flavor remover. If I couldn't convince my mom to pack a Dutch loaf sandwich that day, I'd dutifully produce my 35 cents at the end of the line. It was my introduction to food so nice, you pay for it twice.

Pumpkin Pie Etiquette: Cool Whip it, Cool Whip It Good!

If you don't believe pie can be polarizing, just casually mention how much you LOVE pumpkin pie at your next family gathering. Watch the camps form. The world can be divided into those who enjoy the complex texture and heady spice blend of pumpkin pie, and those who will let you know which 10 types of pie are so much better. At least you didn't say "rhubarb" with a straight face.

The lack of understanding about pumpkin pie begins with the cooking instructions. This is not a pie you can stick in an oven for a few minutes to reheat, or simply thaw and serve. A frozen pumpkin pie goes in the oven at 325 degrees and stays there for about three days. Judgment calls must be made about the crust and the filling's jigginess. Spice levels are also a consideration, from waving a can of pumpkin pie spice over the puree to emptying the contents of the spice rack.

A spicy pumpkin pie needs something to mellow it out, and that something is often whipped cream. This is where the Cool Whip meets the road. Non-believers may want to turn away, but proper pumpkin etiquette requires a ratio of one tub to one slice. I don't make the rules, people.

Battle Of The Network Stars: My Money Was Always On Mr. Kotter.

Most children of the 1970s had no idea how television studios actually worked, we only know they did. Fonzie was the coolest cat in three counties, but we didn't know Henry Winkler. Mr. Kotter was the greatest teacher ever, but we couldn't pick Gabe Kaplan out of a line-up. Television stars weren't like movie stars. Television stars lived in little boxes in our living rooms, and showed up every week like clockwork to get into one half-hour jam or another.

All of these stars collided on a series of prime-time specials called "Battle of the Network Stars". Our favorite characters from all three networks would suit up at a track and field set somewhere and compete against each other. If nothing else, it was a chance for teenage boys to see Janet from Three's Company or Daisy from Dukes of Hazard in swimsuits. I'm sure there was something in it for the ladies as well, but does Arnold Horshack count?

The chances of reviving Battle of the Network Stars with today's casts are slim. Studios have too much invested in their talent to let them trade paint with other actors. One twisted ankle or bad javelin throw and there goes Gray's Anatomy for a year. Maybe some executive will let them join the circus, but that's another story.

K-Mart's Arcade Emporium: Force Another Nickel In.

In the early 80s, the manager at our local K-Mart saw dollar signs in the form of Pac-Man, Dig Dug, and the Karate Champ. He converted a little-used back room into a video game arcade, allowing parents to follow the Blue Light and enjoy a sub sandwich while we saved the universe. Instead of quarters, the machines only accepted special tokens we had to buy at fair market value. At one point, it was six tokens for a dollar.

While many of us followed the rules and used the tokens to chop-sock our way through Karate Champ or blow the Space Invaders to smithereens, a new crop of petty criminals emerged. SOMEONE, ahem, discovered that certain machines would also accept nickels with the right amount of enthusiasm. Instead of spending a dollar on 6 lousy plays, the going rate became 20 plays for a buck. Take THAT, Blinky, Pinky, Inky, and Clyde!

Eventually, the K-Mart employee stationed closest to the arcade discovered our crime ring, after clearing out hundreds of nickels from the machines one night. Within a few weeks, the entire arcade was gone, along with our high scores and unused tokens. Crime may not pay, but it CAN rack up a lot of extra turns.

Moon Shoes: On The Wrong Side Of Orthopedic History

Many toys in the 60s and 70s only lasted as long as the lawsuits were still pending. There were heavy hitters like Lawn Darts, Clackers, and Creepy Crawler Thingmakers, but a few mainstream toys also made the list, like Hula Hoops, Slip and Slides, and strap-on roller skates. The one I wanted most as a kid sounded just as bad on paper as it did in reality. Duplicating the effects of zero gravity would have been a snap with a pair of Moon Shoes.

Original Moon Shoes used exposed metal compression springs to provide lift and bounce to perfectly good sneakers. The idea was to make a series of hops, hopefully followed by a series of safe landings. Good luck with THAT project. Assuming you didn't crush the compression springs outright, the minimal boost would usually be followed by an ankle-busting skid. I seriously doubt Neil Armstrong experienced that much pain on Apollo 11.

Eventually, the toy company powers-that-be got hip to the Moon Shoe jive. After a brief recall for security theater purposes, a new generation of Moon Shoes appeared with state-of-the-art plastic suspension. The exposed metal compression springs became a distant memory about how Daddy got that scar. At least no Creepy Crawlers were harmed.

Fusicte outo⁓ triólutid a vern tons and loaded lomely's kiitchen wall.

The Family Wall Phone: My Life Is An Open Book And Tangled Cord

A telephone in the early 1970s took two forms. One was a clunky floor model with a heavy handset and a rotary dial. The other was mounted to the kitchen wall and had a long, curly cord just waiting to kink up. It MIGHT have been one of those new-fangled touch-tone models, but most of us weren't the Rockefellers. We had one communal phone and absolutely no Cone of Silence.

This lack of privacy suited my dad, the founder of the phone feast, just fine. He didn't like talking on the phone much to begin with, and the phone was usually the first thing he threatened to remove if we pushed the issue. On the other hand, we kids couldn't wait to start long conversations with our friends or be the first to answer the ring. Eventually, we learned how to live in our own little world where no one actually cared what we said. What stayed within 5 feet of the kitchen phone STAYED near the kitchen phone.

The wall-mounted landline phone remained a fixture in many houses until the first affordable cordless phones appeared on store shelves. We could now take our conversations to the next level while hiding out in the bathroom. At least we gave our neighbors with shortwave radios something to chew on.

64 Crayons And Nothing On: The Smell Of Burnt Umber In The Morning

In the beginning, crayons came in boxes of 8, barely covering the basic rainbow, plus black and white. White actually became a rainbow of its own as it steadily picked up all the other colors. We thought we were happy enough with the Basic 8, but then Crayola moved up exponentially, releasing boxes of 16, then 32 crayons. Faces no longer had to be yellow or brown– they could be shades of pink or peach. Shades could be raw, normal, or burnt. Subtlety was finally possible.

32 seemed to be the ceiling in the crayon world, but then Crayola released its magnum opus. The 64-crayon box, with a built-in sharpener. The sharpener meant we no longer had to use crayons worn to the nubs for delicate work. White could be restored to white, not the speckled egg tone it affected later in life. We suddenly had Raw Umber and Burnt Umber, Raw Sienna and Burnt Sienna. Apparently, no one at the factory knew how to cook umber properly.

The 64 box remained the Cadillac of crayon collections until companies started releasing exotic fare such as metallics and skin tones. Magic Markers and gel pens also got in on the multicolor act, allowing for fancy tricks like blending and shading. Just hand me the one called "Red" and I'll kick it old school.

An Amusing Little Chicken Finger: The Indignities Of The Kid's Menu.

On those rare occasions when our family would leave the canned corn and meatloaf behind and visit a local restaurant, Mommy and Daddy were handed the keys to the culinary kingdom. THEIR menu included exotic and adventurous foods, including succulent prime rib, delectable seafood, mouth-watering Italian dishes, and spicy Indian fare.

The kids got the kid's menu. A hot dog. A few chicken fingers. A hamburger. Some fries. Coke. It didn't matter if the sign on the door read "Pat's Legendary Steakhouse" or "Wong Foo's Chinese Palace", the kid's menu read "Hot Dog. Chicken Fingers. Hamburger. Fries. Coke". I understand why this kept happening INTELLECTUALLY, but understanding alone wasn't putting the good stuff in my belly.

Eventually, I reached the age of consent and was finally allowed to look at the regular menu. I was free to order all of those delicious, cheesy, spicy foods that eluded me all those years. But years of conditioning had done their worst. I couldn't believe it myself when the words "Hamburger. Fries. Coke." came out of my mouth. I didn't even get to solve the maze on the back.

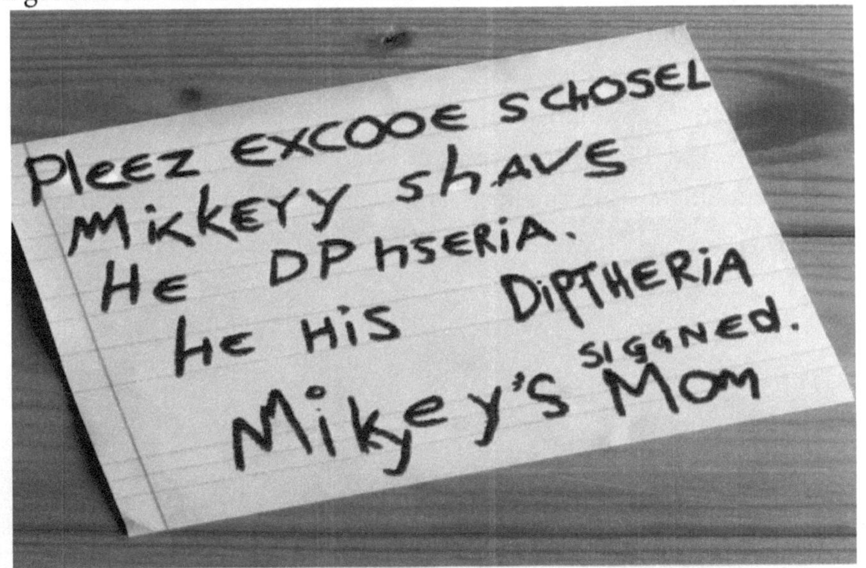

Dropsy, Scurvy, and Typhoid: It's All In Mom's Note

For a handful of Gallant-grade students, there was a sheet of paper with a gold star to celebrate their perfect attendance. For the rest of us, there were "Mental Health Days". The school system built five days of excused absenteeism into the student handbook, and who was I to go against the student handbook? It helped to have an understanding young mother who didn't mind having an extra pair of hands when she had a crafting deadline to meet or a freelance babysitting gig.

The timing of these mental health breaks was critical. They couldn't be on a test day, the weather had to be near-perfect, and any make-up work would have to be manageable. Other than that, it was Bob Barker, The Young and the Restless, and a trip to the park for THIS guy. I could have just as easily been Mod Podge, Plaster of Paris, and wedding chocolates, however. The price of freedom was often crafting or babysitting.

Everything hinged on the one crucial piece of information the school required. Mom and I realized the actual disease didn't matter, like the first three minutes of COPS or the last three minutes of "Jerry Springer". We would look up the most obscure medical conditions from world history and she would sign the note. I'm a proud survivor of laughing disease, smallpox, and pleurisy. Are telethons still a thing?

An Ohio State Yankee In Bear Bryant's Court: Read The Room, Son.

Few people spit in God's eye and live to talk about it. Professional football was the default setting in the frozen tundra of northeast Ohio in the 1970s. We had two decent pro teams to follow, along with whatever Terry Bradshaw was doing in Pittsburgh. College football was more of an afterthought. We had Ohio State, and…and…others. Ohio State had one legendary rival, the University Of Michigan. It also had one infamous coach named Woody Hayes. Coach Hayes was no Amos Alonzo Staggs, for sure.

So when I moved to Alabama in 1986, I was still filled with child-like enthusiasm for Ohio State. I failed to realize that college football is king in Alabama, and Paul "Bear" Bryant was the greatest head coach of all time. Ohio State happened to be facing the University of Alabama one weekend, and I felt honor-bound to start trash-talking at my job It was the proper thing to do whenever Ohio State squared off against Meat Chicken.

The minute I stopped talking smack about Alabama, I felt the air leave the room and my soul leave my body. I had just shot Bambi's mother, and a posse was forming. A kind older lady pulled me aside and taught me about the Alabama football birds and bees. All I can say now is "Roll Tide!" and "Thank you for not murdering me in my sleep".

Billboards, Old Homesteads, and Road Quality: How Alabamians Give Directions

Plugging coordinates into a GPS system is a nice perk. Plotting out a route through an online mapping service is good. But they pale in comparison to asking an Alabama native how to get to the nearest Wal-Mart. The safest bet is to find an individual local– a cashier, a gas station attendant, a waitress. If two or more are gathered together, none of them will agree on the best way to get there. Thank them kindly and walk back briskly.

A certain personal injury attorney is on a mission to install one of his billboards every mile on the mile. I won't say his name, but he wants you to call him, Alabama. My favorite way of giving directions is to tell drivers how many of his signs they'll pass on the way, including the ones he's deliberately hung upside down to match the orientation of accident victims.

Other popular choices are obscure references to obscure landmarks. "You take a right at the old Wilson place and then a hard left where the Piggly Wiggly used to be." Someone once told me to take the first GOOD LOOKING blacktop road. As they say, if you don't know where you're going, any road will take you there.

Karaoke Actually Means "Open Bar": A Celebration At The Love Shack.

It was the middle of the 80s, and a high school friend told me about a wondrous new thing he had just witnessed the night before at his favorite watering hole. You could choose a favorite song, stand in front of a microphone, and instantly alienate everyone else in the room. It was called "karaoke". Not being a singer myself, I really struggled to cough up an enthusiasm hairball for this successor to dwarf tossing.

A few years later, another friend took me out to a local bar for Karaoke Night. My first selection ever was Elvis Presley's "Marie's The Name (of his latest flame)", and it seemed to go okay. A few rounds later, I'm taking on Motown, Stax, and Creedence Clearwater Revival. I became a convert, and maintained that lifestyle for 20 years after that. I even got to be a karaoke host a few times. I've got friends in low places, I've spent jukebox money at the Love Shack, and I don't even call people by their names.

I miss the earliest versions of karaoke, when singers relied more on liquid courage than actual ability. One night, I saw a guy belting out Don Henley's "All She Wants To Do Is Dance" just before falling over the speaker and monitor. I thought all SHE wanted to do was dance, but all HE wanted to do was WALK.

Love Bites: Dog To Cat Person Conversion Therapy

I've heard that dogs see humans as supreme leaders of the pack, while cats see us as weird hairless cats that haven't learned our place. Dogs play checkers, while cats play with the chess board they just knocked over. Dogs greet you at the door with wild abandon and frenzy. Cats greet you with an intoxicating blend of disdain and disinterest.

I grew up a dog person, and I remember a long succession of German Shepherds, Pomeranians, Poodles, Golden Retrievers, and Bulldogs. I only dealt with other people's cats from a distance, and I never imagined actually taking possession of one. That is until I married a cat person. Our first cat together was a slash course on feline ownership. You place cat on floor YES, you place cat on floor NO. You place cat on floor GUESS SO, get sliced into five sections just like the cartoons.

I've learned to love cats, and no longer in a Stockholm Syndrome sort of way. The three overlords in my house now have settled into an armed truce amongst themselves, and actually allow us to touch them on alternating Tuesdays. I still miss the manic energy of a dog, but there's something to be said for catly dignity. I just say it without direct eye contact.

Stacks Of Moldy Oldies: My Brief Career As A Disk Jockey

For a few brief, shining months in the 90s, I worked the same boards and plugged in the same carts as Wolfman Jack, Dick Clark, and Alan Freed, but on a slightly smaller scale. My job at a local AM radio station was to convince listeners that their favorite Oldies show, Zippo in the Morning, was actually local. I recorded brief weather reports, wrote spots for local advertisers, and occasionally did a live remote broadcast, complete with Zippo swag.

In reality, Jim Zippo lived a comfortable life in Houston, Texas, and I only spoke to him a few times over the phone. If anyone bothered to ask, however, he just left the booth a few minutes ago. Sorry. I still took calls from local listeners who hadn't caught on to the concept of syndication. One caller regularly requested the song "Georgy Girl" by the New Seekers. By regularly, I mean every hour on the hour. My pleas to Houston, Texas fell on deaf ears, although Zippo did play it one time while I was there.

The job ended when the station owner decided there was more advertising money to be made in the service of sports talk shows. There was no American Graffiti melting popsicle moment with the real Zippo, but I still hope a devoted listener finally got his long-distance dedication.

Super Spastic Bubble Classic: Ventilation Is For Sissies

Those of us who missed out on airplane glue at least had a consolation prize in the form of Super Elastic Bubble Plastic. This cosmic goo arrived in a Day-Glo tube, and gave off the best fumes any 8-year-old could hope for. The point was to position a small bead of the goo on one end of a straw and carefully blow into the other end. If all went well, the goo would form a surprisingly sturdy multi-colored balloon.

If things didn't go well, breaches would form along the hull and the mission was doomed. A new bead of Super Goo usually allowed for a do-over. No humanity would be lost. The product's chemical formula was mostly non-toxic and even became a weird form of gum for the brave. It was the fumes generated as it cured that generated all the buzz. Did I just say that out loud?

The original Super Tragic Hubbub Magic eventually disappeared from store shelves as concerned parents did what concerned parents did best. There are modern versions available if you know a guy, but they've been stepped on, man. What's a kid got to do to get his bubble on now?

The Back Of The Station Wagon: It's Not The Heat, It's the Fumidity

The only thing better than riding in the family station wagon to Grandma's house was riding backward in the communal pit in the back. The open floor plan allowed select passengers to roam about the cabin freely, once the captain had issued the "You kids settle down back there right now!" speech. The back became everything from a rumpus room to a picnic area to sleeping quarters. There was no seat belt in sight, either.

The view out the tailgate reminded us of where we'd been, not where we were going. We could watch everything we knew slowly fade into obscurity, or find new and interesting ways to distract the other station wagons behind us on the highway. When it was time to refuel, eat, or use the facilities, one of the parents would release the gate and let the cattle out. Life was good in the back of the station, except for one glaring design flaw. The exhaust pipe.

The exhaust pipe on a 1970s land barge couldn't help but funnel fumes back into the cabin. We weren't just getting sleepy organically, we had a little help from Mother Carbon Monoxide. The combination of heat and fumes took a lot of the wind out of our sails long before we ever pulled into Grandma's well-ventilated driveway.

Garanimals: Comic Book Clothing For The Stylistically Impaired

Once a year, our trip to the local mall had a higher purpose. It was time to buy new Brady Bunchwear for school, and Mom had the magic Sears card in her purse, next to the half stick of gum and perfume. We would usually get two pairs of Wrangler jeans, which took the rest of the school year to break in, if ever. Pull-over shirts with zippers would be next, followed by a few Day-Glo button-up shirts from the Joanne Worley collection.

Sears introduced a line of children's clothing that took ALL of the guesswork out of the equation. They were called Garanimals. Garanimals were definitely red, blue, yellow, or green, and were associated with specific zoo animals. The point was to buy blue alligator pants to match the blue alligator shirt, or the yellow giraffe top to coordinate with the yellow giraffe bottoms. Anyone caught wearing red monkey Garanimal pants with green froggy shirts would face the wrath in September.

Garanimals as a fashion statement only lasted a few years, as muted colors that existed in nature became the hippest thing on shelves. Sears itself would also take a hit with shoppers, but not before giving us a chance to give the Wranglers a much-needed breather.

Recipe Renegades In The Sarvice Of The Lard

Getting drunk with the mayor in the middle of the day wasn't in my job description, but it wasn't my fault. Not entirely. The dessert was clearly marked BOURBON Street Pecan Pie, and he did ask for seconds. I found the old Southern cook responsible for the pie and asked her how much bourbon she put in the filling. She said with a smile, "I don't measures, I just pours." Spirit animals show up when you least expect them.

Jerry's Diner was a 24-hour greasy spoon, complete with a legendary lunch and dinner buffet. At the end of the Golden Steam Table lived a fruit cobbler that was 5 percent fruit, 5 percent crust, and 90 percent butter. You could watch the lake form. I met the ladies responsible for that cobbler at a family barbecue, and I asked them how much butter went into those things. The answer was "You really don't want to know."

If cooking is considered art and baking is considered chemistry, then Southern cooking should be considered legalized blasphemy. Recipe books make great housewarming gifts or doorstops, but copious amounts of lard and love make a real biscuit.

A Plank Of Wood, A Cinderblock, And An Audience: Key Ingredients For Committing Evel

Bikes weren't just basic transportation back in the day. They were also currency, status symbols, and opportunities to impress the ladies. These weren't the elite 10-speed models designed for road racing, these were the low-slung, built-to-last, banana-seat street versions built for stunts and unsanctioned BMX competitions.

Within every boy in my block lived the spirit of Evel Knievel, the greatest motorcycle stuntman who ever lived. Evel showed up every weekend on our TVs to jump yet another series of buses, and the landings always provided slow-motion motivation for us. We could pull off the same trick if we just had a proper ramp and nerves of steel. Nerves we had, but a proper ramp, not so much. It was a long wooden plank, supported by a cinderblock or two.

Most of the time, we managed to pull off the jump, with or without other kids positioned under the ramp, but we never did recreate the visuals of Evel's tragic landing at Caesar's Palace. The best we could do was a flat tire and massive apologies to the last volunteer in the landing zone.,

PERMANENT RECORDS
DEPARTMENT

IN SEARCH OF: The "Permanent Record."

A former Vulcan once hosted a series of paranormal investigations called IN SEARCH OF, and one topic he managed to miss was the mythical "permanent record." From the first half-day of kindergarten to the final "what am I even doing here?" days as a Senior, school authorities allegedly maintained a secret file on every student's academic ups and downs. Anything and everything you did within the hallowed halls would be dutifully recorded, and would follow you for the rest of your post-graduate life.

The mere threat of adding a minor infraction to this permanent record was enough to keep most of us in line. Teachers delivered the line "This is going on your permanent record, young man!" with absolutely no hint of deception. Part of their job, after we got on the bus, was to compile a daily list of permanent record addendums. Nothing escaped their steadfast gaze, so you'd better be good for goodness sake.

Years later, I discovered that an adult could formally request a copy of the mythical permanent record for a nominal fee. As it turned out, the reality of the permanent record was nothing like the myth. A few test results HERE, a few report cards THERE. Spock didn't even need to get out of his trailer.

Bathrobes, Paper Plates, Tinsel: An Intro To Church Play Stagecraft

An important requirement for church membership is a willingness to mumble at least one line in a church-sponsored Nativity play. It might just be "Lo, I am but a lowly shepherd, and I am sore afraid!" while pointing towards the sky, but it does move the plot. Costume notes include bathrobes, towel turbans, and untamed Halloween costume beards. Continuity is Job 4.

The other cinematic shorthand involves the use of common household items such as paper plates, Christmas tree garlands, and coat hangers. Without the proper divine headgear, it can be hard to pick out the little cherubs from the rest of the crowd. In my hometown, a local factory produced a gold-colored adhesive tape called Mac Tac, and it was overused with abandon.

My brother once assisted with a special effect surrounding the ascension of Jesus. In reality, "Jesus" stood on the in-floor baptistry cover while an amateur weightlifter pressed and locked it above his head. My brother turned on the blacklight. Jesus ascended 18 inches into the heavens.

Trapper Keepers: Organize Your Files, Store Your Supplies, Block Out The Sun

No back-to-school ritual in the 1980s was complete without the selection of a new Trapper Keeper, the embodiment of "everything in its place and a place for everything." Trapper Keepers were designed specifically to hold the company's other product line called Trappers. They featured a wide range of rad graphics, and had the capacity to store everything from paper to pens to rulers. They were also large enough to block out the sun if necessary.

Trapper Keepers filled the void left behind by pencil boxes and loose-leaf binders, but started to buckle under their own weight by the end of the 90s. Storing and carrying an original Trapper Keeper became a skill all its own. One corner or another was always making unsolicited contact with a doorway or an elbow or something. A Trapper Keeper could easily become a Trapper Spiller if held at the wrong angle.

Although leaner, meaner versions of the Trapper Keeper are still on the market, the originals have largely gone the way of Members Only jackets and parachute pants. Those of us who remember should remain most righteous and totally tubular in their honor.

Are You Ready For Some FOOSBALL? The Non-Athletic Thrill Of Youth Group Competition

Friday night was youth night at my childhood church, which happened to be right next door to my house. This meant time was not a factor—I could stay until the last cookie was eaten and the last ping-pong ball rolled away. In the converted tool and die shop we called the youth center, there were three major entertainment options: Ping-Pong, Bumper Pool, and Foosball. To this day, I have no idea what the rules of Bumper Pool actually were.

Foosball was where the action was. While the adults sat around drinking coffee from the avocado green urn and filled up on electrocuted hot dogs, the kids congregated in another room and formed foosball alliances. One-on-one play was an option, but two-person teams provided the sort of high-level play our fans had grown to expect. The biggest concession to safety was the institution of a no-spinning rule, the foosball equivalent of restrictor plates.

Even without spiking privileges, several formidable opponents rose from the ranks, and the rest of us watched in wide-eyed wonder at the display of cat-like reflexes on both sides. At least that's how I would write it up for Sports Illustrated, if they ever asked. Meanwhile, to the victor goes the left-over hot dogs.

Ultraman Is Going To Die, And I Just Can't. I Just Can't.

I can't hold the entire staff at Channel 43 responsible for the near-death of Ultraman, but it was a terrible thing to do to a kid. I should back up. Channel 43 was a local UHF channel originally housed in a renovated bowling alley. They showed the usual selection of children's shows, like Little Rascals and Huckleberry Hound, to more adult fare, like Hee Haw and Star Trek. Two shows in particular caught my ten-year-old fancy, and both came from Japan.

Johnny Sokko and His Flying Robot was straightforward enough. A young boy controls a benevolent giant robot with his wristwatch, and together they fight monsters. The second feature was Ultraman, in which a member of an elite police force can summon the life force of an alien to...well...fight monsters. He's on a timer, however, and a yellow warning light blinks when the battery is low.

In one episode, Ultraman ignored the yellow light completely, causing a previously unknown red light to glow. Ultraman was going to die, and a ten-year-old boy was about to lose his mind. Fortunately for both of us, an even bigger Ultraman swooped down and recharged him. I had to settle for pizza rolls.

In Defense Of NECCO Wafers: I Am But A Small Voice.

Conveniently timed just before Halloween, lists of the worst candies ever created magically appear across the Internet. The lists almost always contain heavy hitters like black licorice, Circus Peanuts, and Peeps. Sometimes those peanut butter chews in orange and brown wrappers will appear, along with Good & Plenties and Dots. I tend to throw Milk Duds under the bus myself.

But there's one perennial member of that group I believe deserves a little more respect and understanding, and of course I'm referring to the original gangsta, NECCO wafers. NECCO wafers have apparently been around since the dawn of Man, or at least the 1830s. These coma-inducing slugs of sugary love were enjoyed by my parents, their parents, their grandparents, and even the ones not covered in the Ancestry subscription. NECCO wafers survived the Civil War, and all other wars after that. Can any of us make the same claim?

NECCO wafers get a bum rap because they are so extremely primal. It's sugar, flavored with whatever herbs were available then, and pressed into bite-size portions for good pioneer children. When you crunch up a NECCO wafer, you're experiencing the same disappointment and cringe as your forefathers, and THAT alone should keep it off the list.

Children's Public Television: Is It Too Late To Be A ZOOM Kid?

While the Big Three networks may have owned Saturday mornings, and local channels featured shows like Captain Kangaroo, Romper Room, and the New Zoo Review, public television managed to win the hearts and minds of "today's young people." Mister Roger's Neighborhood, Sesame Street, and The Electric Company was where it was at, baby. Easy Reader, back me up on that.

Sesame Street held the high ground, with its sometimes frenetic pace and clever blend of human and felt-based characters. From an obsessive-compulsive blue cookie junkie to grocery store owners who should have lived forever, Sesame Street hit just right. The Electric Company was a worthy upgrade, with live-action skits featuring Rita Moreno and Morgan Freeman delivering the linguistic goods without insulting our fledgling intelligence.

The show I really wanted to be on was ZOOM, with an evolving cast of Boston-area kids spending time showing other kids the coolest tricks ever. I still speak fluent Ubby Dubby, and I also do that weird swirly thing with my arms and elbows. I may not remember passwords or phone numbers, but I do remember one zip code: OH two ONE three FOUR! Send me to ZOOM!

Stays Soggy In Milk: The One About Breakfast Cereals.

Oats, corn, wheat, and sugar: The building blocks of any non-nutritious breakfast as a kid. It was always more about the FORM of the flakes, not the substance. Captain Crunch and King Vitamin were essentially the exact same cereal, but with different career paths. Quisp may have come from outer space, but Pebbles came straight out of prehistoric Earth. There was room in the pantry for all of them.

As hard as our parents tried to get us to make the switch to the vitamin-enhanced healthy cereals like Wheaties or Special K, we remained fiercely loyal to the cereal-shaped candy bars guaranteed to shred the roofs of our mouths. I'm looking at YOU, Captain! If we ever did give in and pour a bowl of Colon Blow, the first thing we did was drown it in sugar. Fortified cereals tasted like rust if you didn't.

There were also the stunt cereals, like the oversized Honeycombs and the original ASMR known as Rice Krispies. Cereals with additives, such as marshmallows and raisins, were also a hit, as long as we didn't try to separate the elements. Whoever came out with whole bags of marshmallows or entire boxes of Crunch Berries was a true genius.

Craft Stores: Suburban Head Shops With Floral Tape

After spending my entire childhood with a mother who never met a craft she didn't like, I now have Plaster of Paris, Fun Film, and Mod Podge running through my veins. Mom generally switched between different projects, starting with Plaster of Paris pendants and then moving on to decoupage artworks culled from magazines. She saved the best for last: molded chocolate candies. It was double-boiler heaven for her assistant.

One of her favorite crafts involve the formation of plastic film flowers, using a questionable product called Fun Film. Fun Film was a combination of nail polish and illicit hallucinogens, a cousin to airplane glue and Super Elastic Bubble Plastic. Mom formed each petal and leaf from floral wire, then combined them into flowers using green floral tape. The results were universally impressive, but the contact high was a reward all its own.

Mom usually donated all of her craft projects to the school as fundraisers, but she occasionally sold a few pieces to earn enough money for more supplies. The local craft store became her version of a head shop, checking to see if they were holding any Fun Film or could hook a sister up with some styrofoam. Personally, I thought they stepped on the Mod Podge, man.

Spock Watch, Fred Bread, and Elton John: Facts Left Off The Brochures

With as little context as possible, here are some fast facts left out of my hometown's Chamber of Commerce brochures. An economics teacher used to put study hall violators on Spock Watch. The offender became Spock, and he or she had to report to "Captain Kirk" if a dot in the corner moved. Football legend Larry Csonka's mother used to deliver the mail. We once tried to change our school colors to pink and black, and call ourselves the Stow High Good and Plenties.

Fred Bread was an unwashed gym shirt stored in an abandoned locker and fed bread and water for a year. A librarian once spent an entire morning tracking down "Elton John" for an overdue book. At a talent show, someone swallowed 10 live goldfish before anyone could tell him about the last-minute baby carrot switch. If a carousel horse usually parked outside a McDonald's went missing, they checked the high school's courtyard first.

You can lead a cow up 3 flights of stairs, but you can't lead it back down. Ask me how I know. There was no pool on the roof, but plenty of pool passes to sell. LeBron James destroyed one of our basketball hoops. Someone carjacked a garbage truck and went on a rampage. At least that one was captured on video.

FROZEN CUSTARD

Frozen Custard Stands: Where God Gets His Ice Cream

If there was a downside to living 300 yards from a legendary local frozen custard stand, I never found it. The owners of Stoddard's had three frozen custard machines custom built to churn twice as slow as the competition, which meant a lot more butterfat and a whole lot less air whipped into the mix. Three machines also meant three flavors, which were routinely chocolate, vanilla, and a Flavor of the Day. The flavor of the day was a true Mystery Date– it could be a dream (blueberry), or a dud (butter rum).

Until the Internet allowed the flavor of the day to be discoverable, part of the fun was the 300 yard dash from my house. The pace would change according to the contents of the sign. If it was banana or strawberry, it became a gallop. If it was a less enticing flavor, it was a saunter. I was always envious of the older neighborhood kids who got to work at the custard stand, because legend had it they were allowed to eat their mistakes. Did someone say "Oops"?

Because the factory responsible for God's ice cream burned down in 1949, those machines were babied beyond belief. I also have a deliberately dim memory about challenging ourselves to order the worst thing possible. Unless someone else orders a butterscotch slushy, I'm still claiming the title.

A Vision In Black and White: The Generic Food Craze

My childhood grocery store surprised us all by installing new food aisles in the late Seventies. Soon, the shelves were filled with a new concept in no-frills grocery shopping: generic food. Instead of Kool-Aid or Lay's, budget-conscious shoppers could now put "drink mix" or "potato chips" in their carts. The packaging went beyond minimalism. The containers were white, with simple black lettering. You wanted corn chips, you got "corn chips".

While the generic food craze had a boffo first act, with cans and bottles and boxes flying off the new shelves, the flaws in the "ointment" soon became apparent. To put it mildly, quality was Job 4. In order to maximize profit and minimize food cost, the powers-that-be running Generic Town simply found third-tier food manufacturers willing to produce a cookie-like product, sir. Generic tortilla chip bags contained corn chips over there, clumps of nacho cheese powder over there, and all the flavor you've come to expect from cardboard.

The generic food craze did not last long, fortunately. The novelty had worn off, and customers on a budget began investing in store brands and off-brands with slightly higher production values. I won't forget the brief, shining moment when generics were actually boss, however.

The Projector Sector: Fraternity, Equality, Visibility

One of the best days at school began when the TV cart entered the room, the shades were pulled, and the lights went off. This meant 29 out of 30 students would soon be enjoying an episode of Sesame Street, ZOOM, or The Electric Company. The other kid became a deputy of the audio-visual squad, otherwise known as the Projector Sector.

Due to the uncertainties of UHF reception, our only hope of cutting through the snow and static was a classmate and an indoor antenna. He would perform an intricate set of moves while perched on a desk not engineered for interpretive dance. The picture would fade in and out until the teacher determined a sweet spot. While the rest of us watched Mister Rogers toss his shoe, the Projector Sector volunteer bravely manned his post.

Whether it was waiting for the beep of a sputtering slideshow or dutifully wheeling an overhead projector from classroom to classroom, those of us on the audio-visual squad still have fond memories of serving both Man and Seventies technology.

Atomic Fireballs: The First Cryptocurrency

For those who believe that cryptocurrency includes names like Bitcoin, Doge, and Ethereum, allow me to introduce you to a cinnamon-flavored jawbreaker known as an Atomic Fireball. Atomic Fireballs could be purchased by the each or in bulk at all the discerning candy stores in my hometown. To the rest of the world, Atomic Fireballs may have been a pact between the Devil and the town dentist, but to us they were a vital part of the schoolyard shadow economy.

You could always trade Atomic Fireballs for other types of candy, trading cards, or even cinnamon toothpicks, the legal loophole around the "no gum in class" edict. There were no set exchange rates, just whatever the market would bear. Inevitably, a few Atomic Fireball robber barons with more indulgent parents or better candy store connections took over most of the action. I'm still into Big Chuck for twenty large.

Atomic Fireballs eventually lost their cache as more and more dealers became users, and we found other commodities to exchange. Wacky Packs, anyone?

We're Mad, We're Cracked, We're Wacky: Subversive Comic Books That Shaped Us

The year is 1970, and a young boy from the suburbs of Akron, Ohio discovers a comic book that would change his life forever. It was called Mad Magazine, and its snarky tone and sensory overload artwork left Richie Rich and Archie in the dust. Mad Magazine introduced pre-teen boys to R-rated movies and edgy song parodies and spies going against spies. The movie parody in this issue happened to .be about "Patton", and it would be years before I could actually see the real thing.

After getting comfortable with Mad's stickers, fold-ins, and Don Martin's whatever that was, it was time to branch out. Mad's main competitor for the hearts of nerds was called Cracked. Cracked Magazine was a little less sophisticated than Mad. It didn't rely on subtleties or clever word play. Cracked understood its key demographic, and became the Mad magazine you got when mom wouldn't let you have the real deal.

The grocery store shelf cousin to both magazines was a series of trading cards called Wacky Packages, or Wacky Packs for those in the know. Wacky Packs used garish comic book imagery to mock real products, like A-Jerks Cleanser or Hungry Jerk pancake mix. Wacky Packs eventually buckled under the weight of trademark infringement, but it was fun while it lasted.

BOOKSTORE

The School Bookstore: A Janitor's Closet Filled With Wonders

The annual back-to-school trek to stores like K-Mart and Sears was supposed to meet all of our clothing, Trapper Keeper, pencil box, and crayon needs, but sometimes protractors and compasses just happen. Sometimes, erasers just fall off—the universe can be cruel that way.

For those first-grade world problems, there was a solution: the school bookstore. The school bookstore only existed for a few short minutes before classes started, so timing was everything. It was a converted janitor's closet, and was usually manned by the giants of the elementary school, sixth graders. Need a new eraser? Five cents, please. A little light on the wide ruled paper and fat pencils? Ten cents, please. It was a racket for sure, but the bookstore could still hook a brother up.

I actually got to work a shift or two at the bookstore, as a worldly sixth grader. With minimal on-the-job training, I managed to serve the public good with a positive attitude and the promise of a free lunch for my efforts. Not bad for a 15 minute gig.

Fruit Float, Fruit Float, Fruit Float: If Jello And Yogurt Had A Love Child.

In the world of food fads and trends, there are perennial favorites that disappear without warning, like Maple Nut Goodies, and food lab experiments that were born to die. Libby's Fruit Float was definitely in that second camp. Fruit Float was a concentrated slurry of a dairy product, sweetener, thickening agents, and real fruit pieces, typically strawberries, pineapples, and peaches.

Consumers would pour this starter pack into a large bowl and mix it with cold milk. This was where the magic happened. After a few minutes in the fridge, it would congeal into a creamy treat somewhere between Jello pudding and yogurt. Essentially, it tasted like what you HOPED yogurt would taste like, but didn't.

The promotion of Fruit Float consisted of commercials challenging people to say Fruit Float three times fast, which in my mind is not the best quality of a brand name. "I dare you to pronounce this stuff!" The product itself was only on store shelves for about a year or two before it disappeared without ceremony. There are many of us old-timers who would still like to watch it wiggle, and finally become The Blob in a bowl.

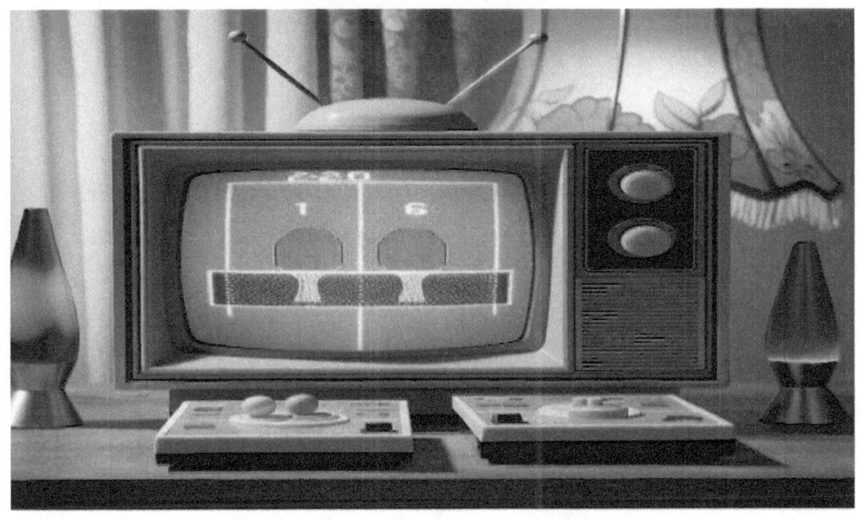

Merlin and the Bliptones: Kicking It Retro-School

In a world where Grand Theft Auto is no longer just a felony, it's hard to believe that children of the Seventies were highly entertained by a single electronic blip. We sent that blip flying across the TV screen in Pong. We fired blips at low-rez Space Invaders. Blips turned big Asteroids into little Asteroids. We even ran a blip across a "football field" until we heard the buzzy chirp of a victory march.

For the hipper-than-thou crowd with indulgent parents, there were home video consoles with names like Atari, Coleco, and Intellivision. For the rest of us, there was a local department store with those consoles positioned just out of reach on endcaps. We would take turns risking life and limb for a few precious moments of playtime. Inevitably, what started with Pac Man eventually became Blip Dude at Christmas.

One of the holy grails of electronic games was Merlin, a combination of Simon, Tic-Tac-Toe, and a Magic Ring puzzle. Merlin looked like something Spock would use to detect alien lifeforms, but it checked a lot of our entertainment boxes. If you had three hours to kill and the patience of a saint, you could actually program it to play Jingle Bells. It also reminded us how pointless Tic-Tac-Toe really was, but at least we didn't have to dangle from a store shelf just to play it.

Superballs: The Juicy Fruit of Seventies Toys

There's a reason why Superballs of old rarely became old Superballs. They performed their job TOO well.

It all started with a commercial demonstrating a revolutionary rubber ball forged under fifty thousand pounds of pressure at a mysterious toy factory. They even had a name for its life force: Zectron. Once a Superball started bouncing, whether under a table, down the stairs, or off the top of a building, it never stopped bouncing. In fact, it seemed to pick up steam.

Every rubber ball ever made before 1964 paled in comparison to the Superball. Using a Superball to play Jacks was completely out of the question. It only took a slight miscalculation for a Superball to break free and treat the entire room like Godzilla treated Tokyo.

The main reason most Superballs had the shelf life of Juicy Fruit gum was the overwhelming temptation to test them out from the highest point a ten-year-old could reach, usually a bedroom window or a garage. That trick worked once, and we all got to watch our Zectron-enhanced Superballs bounce down the driveway, never to be seen again.

Monster Chiller Horror Theater: The Supe's On In Cleveland

In order to fill the air with reruns of Gilligan's Island or The Brady Bunch, local television stations in the Seventies had to make a package deal with the studio devils. They could get the rights to a few popular sitcoms or cartoons or Westerns, but they also had to accept thousands of Grade Z horror movies and obscure Hollywood titles as well. The stations usually showed the good shows when they knew kids would be watching, and held off on the schlock until after the late night news.

This is why many mild-mannered program directors like Marty Sullivan from WUAB in Cleveland would become hosts of ultra-low budget horror shows. Sullivan himself donned a set of pajamas emblazoned with an S, and became Superhost. If a movie featured wasp women or 50 foot tall men or radioactive bacteria, it found a home on his Saturday afternoon show.

The show's opening was pure Cleveland humor gold. In his haste to change into his Super Host costume, Marty drops a gold-plated Chuck Taylor tennis shoe. When an innocent bystander picks it up, he grabs it and yells "GIMME DAT SHOE!" Sigh, the price we paid for Hogan's Heroes and Yogi Bear.

The Fourth Grade Skillset Not On My Linked In Profile.

Ventriloquism. What was the thinking here? Much like algebra, I've never had to avoid moving my lips in a dark alley, but that didn't stop me from ordering the "how to throw your voice" pamphlet and learn how to replace half the alphabet with either D or T. My dummy didn't blink, turn its head, or deliver snappy punchlines. It moved its lips up and down, the one thing I wasn't allowed to do myself.

Walking on stilts. Riding a unicycle was a skill. Juggling was a skill. I envied those who could do both at the same time. Following a short learning curve, walking on stilts was just a matter of deciding to do it. Maybe one kid in a thousand got to try those circus stilts that shot up 20 feet in the air. The rest of us could only manage a two foot lift, until it became a 6 inch slog on soaking wet ground.

Magic. David Blaine performs magic. David Copperfield performs magic. The best a kid could do was not get in the way of a self-working gimmick. The real trick was finding what the professionals called "patter". As much stage fright as I had, it felt like I had finally combined ventriloquism with magic after all. No lips dared to move during my attempts at patter.

The Back Room Of Spencer's Gifts: Remember What The Dormouse Said

The local shopping mall in the 70s was the best place to find cookies, clothes, summer sausage kits, shoes, and weird orange drinks under one roof, but cool kids who knew what time it was headed straight for the alternative nation known as Spencer's Gifts. The front half of Spencer's played it straight, with gag gifts featuring rubber dog poo competing for shelf space with snarky coffee mugs and greeting cards for relatives with an actual sense of humor.

The back room of Spencer's was where suburban boys and girls first tasted the day-glow wild side. Harsh fluorescent lighting was replaced with a thing called "black light." Black light gave anything remotely white a radioactive sheen, and there were dozens of posters featuring forbidden fruits such as Grateful Dead artwork and Pink Floyd album covers. The unmistakable scent of patchouli incense wafted over us.

The sensory overload continued with strobe lights, plasma displays, and light organs that reacted to music. Lava lamps and black lights were a match made in hippie heaven. The trickiest part was to recover from this contact high before Mom whisked us off to the matinee movie. Star Wars, I KNOW what you're doing now, and I LIKE it.

Amaze Your Friends For Just Shipping And Handling

There's a reason why this country hasn't been overrun by 7-foot tall, life-like monsters, and it can be found in the back of old comic books. Once you get past the fake Utopia of Sea Monkeys (spoiler alert: brine shrimp) and quit trying to make smoke from your fingertips, the monsters and cardboard submarines took over. Your own personal Frankenstein was only a dollar thirty-five away from fruition.

The time between ordering your new friend and its arrival in your mailbox was the longest in recorded history. How is the mailman even supposed to get a seven foot tall monster out of the truck and into your room? Did it have enough to eat, and could it breathe? As it turned out, the whole "creature" managed to fit in one business-size envelope.

Truth in advertising is a movable feast, especially when it comes to ads in the back of comic books. My new life-like monster turned out to be a 7-foot long sheet of plastic, accompanied by a balloon with Frankenstein's face on it. Once folded like the Shroud of Turin, my 3 and a half foot buddy didn't exactly amaze any of my friends. MOM thought it was funny.

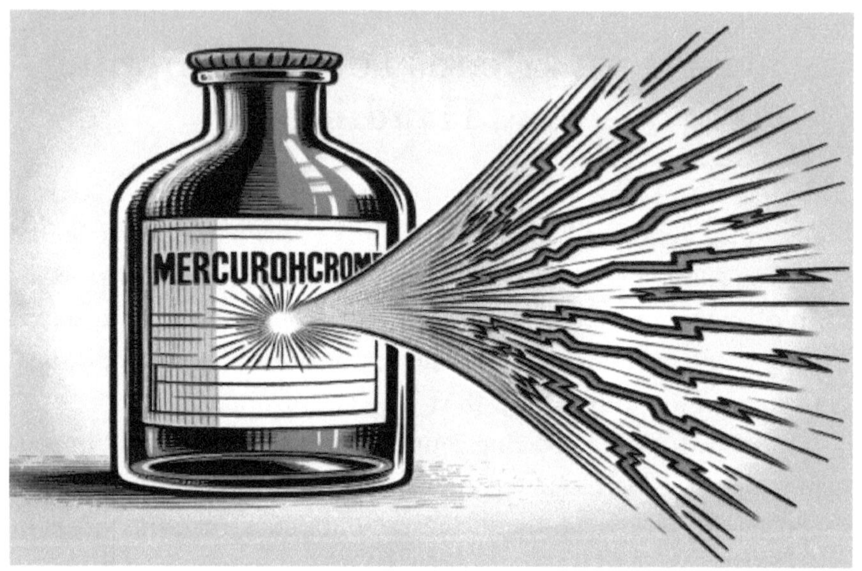
MERCUROHCROME

This May Sting A Little: The Lie That Was Mercurochrome

As most of us can attest, these knees were made for skinning, and that's just what they did. Open wounds and childhood were the default setting, from road rash to trips on the playground. The next step in the semi-healing process was always a memorable disinfection ritual with products Mom always seemed to have on ready-five status.

The first was Bactine, whose major selling point was its relatively pain-free nature. A little squirt of Bactine in the field was good enough for most incidents. The bump up for more serious abrasions was hydrogen peroxide, which might have stung a little bit, but the fascinating foaming action made up for it. It was just fun to watch.

Things took a definite turn for the worse when Mom produced a bottle of furniture stain/paint remover called Mercurochrome. Mercurochrome was mercifully removed from store shelves eventually, but when it was the king of disinfectants, the screams could be heard for miles. It didn't come to play, and many of us wore the orange tattoo as a badge of courage.

Blister Pack In The Sun: The Kid-Friendliest Toy Aisle Ever

Every self-respecting department store had a juvenile version of Mecca known as the toy section. The instant a family entered the store, the children set a new land speed record to get there. Most of the aisles featured brands such as Mattel, Hasbro, and Kenner, and price tags such as $14.95 and $29.95. This is where the phrases "maybe for your birthday" and "make sure you tell Santa" were born.

Meanwhile, there was an entire aisle in the toy section that gave children of all ages and tax brackets hope. Racks of toys protected by blister packs were hung by the endcaps with care, hoping parents with a little disposable income soon would be there. The blister pack toys included Whizzers, Jacks, Uno cards, and the ultimate childhood hallucinogen, Super Elastic Bubble Plastic.

The blister pack aisle rarely had recognizable brand names, and the price tags often read one dollar or less. We may not have been able to take home a Star Wars model or a Toss Across, but there was every chance we could leave the store with a yo-yo or a box of caps. If I had a hammer...

NEW!
NEW!
NEW
NEW AND
IMPROVED!

It's Going In The Cart: The Evil Seductress Known As "New And Improved"

My dad rarely did the official grocery shopping in our house. Mom was the one who kept track of our inventory, clipped the appropriate coupons, and ran the gauntlet every week. Dad had more of a visual, impulsive shopping style, one that could be heavily influenced by three words: New and Improved. If the package contained those three words ANYWHERE, it was going in the cart. We didn't like Life cereal? Too bad, it was new and improved.

There have always been professionals who get paid the big bucks to convince us little people we need to improve ourselves whenever possible. Why settle for hamburgers when ribeye steaks lived right next door? Why settle for the old and regular when a shiny new and improved version was on full display? These masters of manipulation certainly found their mark whenever Dad decided to go shopping.

I have to be honest and admit that "New and Improved" works on me, too. When I see the new packaging, I immediately become a food critic. What exactly did they do to improve version 2 point O's newness? Were they holding back a little when they released the original? The fate of many potato chips and breakfast cereals hangs in the balance.

TODAY

There's A Day For That

I happen to be the proud owner of the most oxymoronic job title in the world- a professional poet. Historically, this has proven to mean I'll be long gone before the check for the pizza arrives. We poets live for April, which happens to be National Poetry Month. For a solid thirty days, poetry and poets can roam freely in the streets, without calling their parole officers or violating restraining orders.

April also happens to be National Coffee Month, which makes some sort of symbiotic sense to me. Coffeehouses were generally the first venues to embrace poets, so I can see sharing a month with the hands that feed us. All this talk about national months got me to thinking, though. You have to figure that for every month that makes sense (Black History Month, AIDS Awareness Month, Women in Sports Month, etc.) there must be hundreds that are best described as answers to obscure trivia questions. Creating a new 'Month' must be the bread-and-butter of legislators everywhere. It's got to be the best win/win situation of all time- instant respect for the lawmakers, and recognition of the oft-ignored blue-backed iguana owners of America.

I'd like to know who decides what cause deserves a national Day, Week, Month or Year. The negotiations have got to be the most delicate diplomatic operations in Washington DC: 'You know, Bill, I share your love for the little critters myself, but how about National Wombat DAY? We had to give Senator Jones "National Pantyhose Month", so the calendar's looking a little full right now.' No matter what the occasion, I'd like to think someone is waiting for the Wombat Parade of Heroes to pass by on that special day.

All I know is that next April, I will be sipping my gourmet coffee and working on my next collection of poems. If you care to join me, just remember I like extra pepperoni.

Ritual: The Oldest Word In Any Language

As I sip my first cup of coffee this morning, I'm struck by how much of our lives are defined by ritual. Our morning routines are actually rituals in casual clothing, and without them our day is a goner already.

When I was a child, Sunday morning was the best ritual of all. Mom would start frying bacon on our gas stove around 9 o'clock or so. By the time I rolled out of bed, it would reach the gurgling and splattering stage. The sun would be streaming through our dining room window, and the air felt different than other days. As the bacon continued to fry, my mother would start boiling hot tea in a dented aluminum pot set aside for such a purpose. There was rarely any sense of urgency on Sunday morning- things were going to happen organically, and we understood that.

The bacon would eventually become these burnt stalks of unidentifiable pork, but I looked forward to each and every piece. Mom would scramble some eggs and fry them in the remaining bacon grease. Our breakfasts consisted of cholesterol, sodium and caffeine, but I wouldn't have traded them for the world. It was a ritual that held us together until it was time for church. To this day, I still ask for burnt bacon wherever I go.

So this morning I drank my coffee, watched a little news and made my way to my new church, in my new life as a grown-up. I realize now that we are all responsible for our own rituals, even if they no longer involve cartoons, dented aluminum tea pots or those who made them possible.

What's Next– Coffee-Flavored Coffee?

I've been on a diet for about 6 months now, which explains why I just finished eating a bowl of coffee almond ice cream. Let he who is without carb cravings cast the first Slimfast can. Speaking of diet drinks, I believe more than a few companies have composed coffee-flavored variations on their standard liquid fare. Oh they try to be so clever by calling it 'mocha', but we see through their little ruse.

Over the years, there have been many attempts to blend coffee with another food or beverage. Some have proven hugely successful, while others have fallen a little short of the glory. Coffee ice cream came straight out of the vat with a halo and a large bow saying 'Buy me, I'm terrific!', while the earliest versions of cold cappucinos played cards on the shelves and said 'When you run out of every other drink in the house, you know where I live.' Times have changed, and now frozen or chilled cappucinos are among the most popular drinks in gourmet coffeehouses.

Sometimes it just comes down to building the perfect beast and waiting for the right consumers to find it.

You Know That We Are Living In A Coffee World

As appealing as it sounds, there is one coffee-enhanced beverage I'm glad hasn't made it onto store shelves-Drew Carey's infamous Buzz Beer. For those of you who missed the show, Buzz Beer came about after one of Drew's cronies started drinking coffee between taste tests. The combination proved to be marketable on the show, but I seriously doubt anyone would actually try to duplicate it in real life. Coffee has been used in a lot of strange concoctions, but beer seems to do best on its own. (At least I won't be polishing off a pint of beer pistachio ice cream any time soon). That's okay, though- it leaves more room in the fridge for my card-playing iced cappucino buddies.

My wife tells me that she's been drinking coffee since she was four years old, and somehow I believe her. It may be the dozen or so cans of Story House gourmet coffee strewn around the house, or it may be the fact that we are already on our third coffeemaker in six years of marriage. We can't leave the local coffeeshop/bookstore without gazing longingly at the top-end cappucino machines and French press carafes on the shelves. You know those oversized bins of whole bean coffee at the grocery store? I'm beginning to think they're actually free gumball machines for coffee fanatics.

My wife says she started her coffee habit by finishing off the dregs of coffee left behind by her parents. My brother started drinking coffee at our mother's funeral. He started off with equal proportions of cream, sugar and coffee, then eventually acquired a taste for the stronger stuff. Being an inveterate hot tea drinker from way back, I still prefer a little cream and sugar in mine. My first real exposure to coffee was not in a cup, but one of those chewy coffee-flavored candies. I took one bite, expecting chocolate, and received a rather abrupt introduction to the world of coffee.

Some say the world is divided into two groups- those who like Neil Diamond and those who don't. I say that the world can be divided in a different way- the world we knew before coffee, and the one we discovered after that first cup. 'Coffee World' is inherently different- life has a few more edges, a little more color. Like any other first experience, you can sense that an invisible border has been irreversibly crossed, but somehow you don't seem to mind the change. Coffee World can be a challenging place sometimes, but its also worth trying all the way to the dregs.

There's Music In That Coffee, Mister

As I settle down to my final cup of coffee for the day, I hear the opening strains of Van Morrison's "Brown-Eyed-Girl" and realize how good life can get. I'm not sure what the most perfect song in the world would sound like, but I think John Prine is going to write it and Van Morrison is going to sing it. If they don't, I'm sure Tom Waits, Bruce Springsteen or Bob Dylan will be on ready five status.

Surprisingly enough, coffee shows up in a lot of memorable songs. Mickey Dolenz promises time for "coffee-flavored kisses and a bit of conversation" in the Monkee's Last Train to Clarksville. Don Williams begins his lonesome day with "coffee black, cigarette" in his country hit Some Broken Hearts Never Mend. Bob Dylan lingers over One More Cup of Coffee before facing (The Valley Below). Oddly enough, I don't believe the Beatles ever mentioned coffee in their music, but one might wonder what was in the cup Paul speaks of in A Day in the Life. Coffee is almost always the one bit of normalcy that creeps into the songwriter's otherwise complicated verses. We can all identify with that desperate search for the waitress, or that early morning jolt of reality only coffee can bring.

For a long time, I thought Van Morrison's Into the Mystic was as close to perfection as anyone could get. Now I'm beginning to think that we are all responsible for writing our own perfect song, one where the verses don't really matter and all our friends know the chorus by heart.

There's A Full-Scale Yemana In Progress– I Repeat, In Progress

Did you know that in 16th century Turkey a man could be fined for not keeping his family coffeepot full? Only a scant 500 years later, a few of us should be arrested for doing just that. Few things disappoint more people in a shorter time than a pot of freshly-brewed bad coffee.

I got to thinking about the ancient Turkish solution to bad coffee, and I realized we actually have a patron saint of tarnished brew- Detective Nick Yemana from the TV sitcom "Barney Miller". Yemana's bad coffee was legendary among his co-workers, and when Jack Soo, the actor who played Yemana, passed away in 1979, the entire cast raised a mug in tribute. So I thought it might prove useful to provide 'Yemana Rights' to anyone accused of serving up less-than-ideal java:

'You have the right to grind your own beans.

Anything you do grind up will be filtered,

and served to you in a court of public opinion.

You have the right to clean water and clean equipment-

if you cannot afford clean equipment, a Mr. Coffee will be issued to you

and charged to Joe DiMaggio's account.

You have the right to ask for a Starbuck's or SBC employee to be near you during questioning. If you cannot find a Starbuck's or SBC employee,

you're not trying hard enough.

Your coffee is presumed drinkable until proven otherwise in a court of law.

Unless, of course, the judge's clerk hands him the wrong mug. You may be toast.

You may have the right to reclaim any article of clothing used as a filter, but the court suggests you consider it an experiment that went horribly wrong.'

I can just see it now. "Coffee Squad", starring retired detective Nick Yemana and his band of cops-on-the-edge. They work 24 hours a day, 7 days a week, protecting the city from bad coffee makers everywhere. 'Boss, we just got a call from the Kinko's on 24th and Main. It sounds like a Code Sanka IN PROGRESS!' 'Bob, you and the new kid take this one. And be sure he gets Yemanaed real good. I don't wanna lose another one on a technicality!'

I'll Have What Niles Crane Is Having

Coffee and television- now there's a combination just waiting to define a generation. 'Oh, these crazy kids, with their...coffee and their...television.' I'm beginning to feel like I've replaced sex, drugs and rock n roll with carbs, caffeine and NPR.

The other day I caught an episode of Seinfeld in which George accepts his date's invitation for late-night coffee, only to discover she actually MEANT it. He assumed 'going for coffee' was a euphemism for a more intimate encounter. "Who drinks coffee at midnight?" he bellowed to Jerry afterwards. I tend to agree with George more and more often these days, which is scary enough. Going out for coffee has become the invitation of choice for a lot of single people I know. It's really the perfect first date setup- intimate but public, non-threatening, non-intoxicating and conducive to making other plans for the evening — or not. It's an equally good setting for a quick getaway.

There is one thing I don't get about coffee shops on television, however. How is it that the most prominent piece of furniture in Central Perk is always available to at least one Friend? Just try that trick at your own neighborhood coffee shop some time. Frasier's Cafe Nervosa is a little better about table-sharing, but I'd like to find a real waiter who knows what my 'usual' is. They say a goldfish's short term memory is so limited that every time he swims a lap, he discovers the castle all over again. I believe that gene has been passed on to an entire generation of coffee shop waiters. Of course, I do get a kick out of seeing Niles' reaction to even the slightest deviation from his usual order. 'You call this a 'whisper'of nutmeg? It's a full-throated SHOUT!'

I hope to find my own Central Perk or Cafe Nervosa someday, but until then I can still enjoy their presence on television. Now for the benediction- May your couch always be empty, and may the waiters all know your first name. Amen.

Cupping May Just Be One Of Those Metaphors

The coffee world's equivalent of a professional wine tasting is called 'cupping', but don't expect to be invited to a local cupping and danish party any time soon. This is a practice best left to the professionals, if the preparation is any indication.

During a cupping session, individual coffees are ground and poured directly into small cups arranged around a large Lazy Susan affair. Hot (but not boiling) water is added, and the entire solution becomes a sort of coffee slurry. There's no fancy brewing or filtration involved- just coffee beans and water. The tasters spend much of their time absorbing the

fragrances of the selected coffees, then proceed to swirl and swish each cup's offerings with all the elan of their wine-tasting counterparts. In general, the tasters are looking for strong flavors and a good mouthfeel. Copious notes are taken, since the economic future of a smaller plantation may hinge on the results.

But in the midst of all this research, I also discovered a life lesson or two. After the ground beans are mixed with water, a thin layer of residue often forms on the surface of the coffee. Tasters know that the coffee's most essential elements can be found underneath, so they will often place their noses directly over the coffee and 'break the crust'. It struck me how often we fail to do that in our own lives. We encounter new people every day, but we somehow forget to 'break the crust' in order to discover their truest qualities. Sometimes it seems our lives run on their own relentless turntables, but it helps to savor the richness of every cup we're presented.

The Mattress King Is Dead, Long Live The Mattress Queen

There's nothing like a good cup of gourmet coffee after the best night of sleep in your life.

I recently had a reason to put that theory to the test.

I've had the same mattress set for about 10 years now. To be even more accurate, I've endured sleeping on a Nerf pancake studded with dog-collar spikes for almost a decade. My wife and I decided it was time to look for a new mattress and box springs.

Long ago, I developed a hard and fast rule about furniture and bedding outlets. I swore I would never shop in any store that featured fictional characters- no Wizards, no Kings, no Elves, nothing of the sort. My a priori salesman was a guy named Chuck, of Honest Chuck's Mattresses and Beyond.

So here we are in the Hall of the Mattress King. Apparently the King was called away on royal business, so we were greeted by his son- the Mattress Duke, as it were. He invited us to try out any bed in the store, which translated to lying fully clothed on a bed while other customers watch the show. My wife and I became a pair of Goldilocks in a giant warehouse of Bear Family furnishings. We finally decided on a firm, but not TOO firm, mattress with a pillow top. In the store, it looked absolutely perfect.

A few days later, the bed of our dreams arrived by a most royal-looking delivery van. The men finished setting up the frame, boxspring and mattress, then had me sign for acceptance. After they left, I was left alone with my first new bed in years. And then I realized why it was so dark in the bedroom. This monolith was literally blocking out the sun. It was as if we rented a bed and they built an apartment around it to keep out the rain. We've now dubbed it Mount Bed-a-Rest.

Oh sure, it's comfortable. We no longer count ceiling tiles to fall asleep- we ARE the ceiling tiles.

As far as the old mattress is concerned, I was really looking forward to a nice Viking funeral, courtesy of the King's coachmen. Instead, it ended up in a new neighbor's apartment 20 feet away. The night it finally showed up in a dumpster was the best night of sleep I ever had.

Coffee-Metrics

I notice that it's now the 21st century and our beloved country is still blatantly non-metric. Oh, we have the occasional two-liter soda bottle or the schizophrenic rulers marked with both inches and centimeters, but for the most part this is a metric-free zone. Look at it this way- entire countries in Europe have converted their money systems to Euros already, and we still have farthings, hectares and fathoms on our books. If nothing else, consider the fact we are about to be lapped by the Canadians on metric conversions. Doug and Bob McKenzie from the Great White North are closer to world unity than we are, eh?

What strikes me as particularly funny is how fast we Murkins converted to coffee-metrics.

Twenty years ago, coffee came in two sizes- small and large. For whatever reason, small was always TOO small and large approached Super Squishee proportions. Mugs, of course, were one size fits all- that is to say, bottomless. Then came the great gourmet coffee explosion of the late 80s and early 90s. The same Americans who had resisted speaking meters and liters into existence could suddenly order short, tall and grande coffees, without even once questioning the etymology. Heaven forbid I should pump three liters of gas into my tank, but give me a grande half-caf skinny soy mocha latte to go please.

I don't know if we'll ever go fully metric in this century, but I think it would be a great cosmic joke if all the gourmet coffeeshops agreed to change their ordering system to something out of the Wizard of Id comic strip. I would just like to hear one person order, in all seriousness, a 'frippin on the jimjam, frappin on the krotz'. I have this sinking feeling I'll hear that long before I know how many kilometers it is to Disney World.

Keef Knows What Time It Is

I believe we need to listen closer to our rock legends. Recently some linguists managed to compile a "Keith Richards to English, English to Keith Richards" dictionary and it turns out he was actually saying something important during interviews. Keith recently suggested that horses basically saved civilization as we know it. Consider all the important battles whose outcomes depended on the skills of men on horseback. Think about all the contributions draft horses made to improving labor. How far would we have gotten in the Old West if it hadn't been for Old Paint getting us there? I believe our beloved Rolling Stone and rehabilitation icon may be onto something here.

But what other discoveries or ideas can be credited with saving civilization from extinction? I got to thinking about that and came up with a few ideas of my own. First off, I think the creation of walls certainly changed things for the better. Dividing ourselves into smaller and smaller social units probably saved our collective sanity. Communal living might have protected early man, but walls provided a sense of 'self', which in turn promoted the formation of towns and cities. Of course you do have the problem of walls failing to live up to expectations- the Great Wall of China, Hadrian's Wall, the Berlin Wall, etc. Perhaps Frost was right when he wrote in his poem Mending Wall: 'Something there is that doesn't love a wall'. Some walls are good at uniting, while others are bent on division.

I also believe the cultivation of coffee has done a lot to define civilization. Coffee is a lingering reminder of the Ottoman Turk empire, which nearly conquered Europe 500 years ago. The exportation of a single coffee plant from France lead to the dominance of South American coffee growers in the world today. Coffee helped to equalize the economic playing field for many smaller countries struggling to find a viable commodity. Coffee was a staple item for settlers and pioneers, not to mention our fighting soldiers. Coffee became a nearly-universal beverage long before Coca-Cola and Pepsi. I'll even bet that coffee fueled more than a few late-night jams featuring Mick, Keith, Ronnie, Bill and Charlie. So it all comes full circle- horses, walls, coffee and Keith Richards. I just know there's a future Jeopardy question in there somewhere.

"You Should Really Try Out For The Olympics, Kid."

I hold coffee, Andy Coiner and Calvin Rydbom partially responsible for my short-lived life of crime- coffee, because it was 20 degrees that night, with a windchill factor of liquid nitrogen, Andy Coiner, because he was just plain wrong, and Calvin Rybom, because he was in the wrong bleacher at exactly the wrong time.

Andy Coiner was a buddy of mine who lived in the city adjoining my hometown. Our schools were notorious football rivals- some of the old-school Cleveland Browns came from these two institutions. Andy was a natural athlete- strong, wiry and basically fearless. In contrast, I was a thinker, not a fighter. Nonetheless, our two teams were playing on the official Coldest Night of the Year. That's where the first leg of the problem started- artificial coffee courage. Andy had a plan.

My brother and I followed Andy through the woods and right up to a large fence surrounding the football stadium. Time for the second leg of the problem- Andy's amazing climbing ability. He shimmied up and over the fence, followed quickly by my brother. I was the last of the Hole in the Head gang left. Enter Calvin Rydbom. It just so happened that the fence was located on the visitors side of things—in other words, MY school's section. Calvin happened to be on the highest bleacher, which meant he had a perfect view of our crime scene. As I struggled in vain to scale the fence, Calvin decided to encourage me in his own fashion. By the time I reached the top, the entire bleacher section was cheering me on. I fell over the fence and landed at the feet of an off-duty police officer. He escorted me to the ticket office, after congratulating me on my Olympic fence-climbing style. My days of crime came to an end that night, but I learned a couple of lessons: not everyone is cut out for criminal work, and always carry a little cash in your socks, just in case Andy gets any more ideas.

So What Have YOU Been Doing?

As I take a few reflective sips of coffee this morning, I'm reminded of an impending personal milestone. For reasons which will soon become apparent, I'm tempted to change that to read 'personal MILLstone'.

Next year will mark my twentieth season out of high school. Of course you realize this means plane tickets, ill-fitting suits, complete memory loss, hotel reservations and an open bar. Guess which one will get my fullest attention. It's not that I'm against the need for class reunions on some intellectual plane, but sometimes I question the wholesale marketing of what may be a rather painful yardstick for some. I anticipate receiving quite a few unsolicited invitations from companies who specialize in class reunions. I have a feeling I'm going to separating a little wheat from a boatload of chaff when January arrives.

At first I feared that no one from my class would even find me. I just knew I'd end up on that collective Wanted Poster you always see in the local newspaper. Now with the glories of the Internet in full bloom, my new fear is that EVERYONE will find me. I can't speak for all of you, but don't you sometimes think of your former classmates as perpetual teenagers? My last contact with 90% of my class was in the years of Reaganomics and fluorescent clothing. I'm not sure I'm ready to meet the modern editions who will show up en masse at the one country club in my hometown.

I just know I'm going to expect parachute pants and leg warmers a-plenty, while the DJ plays Duran Duran and a Flock of Seagulls. As badly as I want to meet the accountants, teachers, housewives and small business owners of today, part of me still wants to crawl back into the 80s womb and talk about Luke and Laura's wedding all night. Nostalgia isn't everything, but sometimes it's the thing that will keep you the warmest.

Finding Your Inner Nuge

A few years ago, I read an article exhorting readers to find their inner Ted Nugent. By that I gathered we should all embrace our inner gun-toting, caveman-thinking, Alpha-male tendencies once in a while. Oh yeah, and while we're at it we should learn three chords on a really loud guitar and play the same four songs until we die and/or retire. I have a sinking feeling the Nuge would have earned the title "Motorcity Madman" whether he was a rock star or a third-shift busboy at Denny's.

Since I have no interest in acquiring cat scratch fever, I have acquired a new hero. I want to get in touch with my inner Kaldi. For those of you who may be unfamiliar with the history of coffee, Kaldi is the fun-loving Abysinnian goat-herder responsible for discovering an elixir we now call coffee. Legend has it that Kaldi was leading some of his charges through a neighbor's field when they came upon a bush bristling with red berries. The sheep began eating these berries in earnest. Kaldi noticed that his sheep began dancing like frat boys on prom night. Never one to pass up an opportunity to ingest something unproven and potentially life-threatening, Kaldi sampled a few berries himself and became the prototype for SBC customers everywhere. He later shared his discovery with some local monks, who refined the process and produced a bitter but drinkable beverage. They noticed that a few sips of this concoction would give them the ability to stay awake during prayers. Ironically enough, a thousand years later we would be drinking the stuff to stay awake through everything else.

The story of Kaldi, Abyssinian ambassador of strong coffee and dancing sheep, may be apocryphal, but I'd still like to glean a few nuggets of wisdom from it anyway. Sometimes in life you just have to take the word of your flock and throw a few red berries down your gullet. Maybe you'll discover a new and exciting beverage for the ages, or maybe you'll discover a new paint thinner. Maybe you'll discover a new beverage AND a paint thinner, who knows? What doesn't kill you just makes you stronger, or at least more awake in church. So raise a mug to the spirit of Kaldi, a man who missed his calling as a kamikaze pilot or rock guitar legend. As for me, I'll have what the sheep are having, thank you very much.

In Space, No One Can Hear Spock Scream

As I pour a fresh pot of coffee down my thermos, I'm reminded of all those thermoses (thermi?) which have come before.

I honestly couldn't say what the very first beverage I ever drank out of a thermos was, but my gut says Kool-Aid. I distinctly remember picking out an Aladdin Partridge Family lunchbox on that inevitable Back to School trek to our local K-Mart. I came ever so close to the outdated Star Trek model, but uncooler heads prevailed. Inside this seemingly indestructible casing was a matching thermos, complete with full-length drawings of Susan Dey, my future wife. I'd never seen a thermos up close before- it was still one of those Space Age deals. I eagerly screwed off the lid... the cup... the lid AND the cup. Darn, those astronauts are clever.

A brand new thermos has one of those distinctive smells, like a new car or grandma's bathroom. I looked at the shiny aluminized innards for a good long while. This thermos and I would share beautiful moments together- a steady companion in the uncertain world of second grade. As long as Lori Partridge was within my grasp, nothing could go wrong.

About twenty minutes later, something went horribly wrong. I grabbed a marble from the floor and casually dropped it down the gullet of my new thermos. In a moment worthy of the second choice Star Trek lunchbox crew, all heck broke loose. The sides of the thermos lining shattered, followed by a sudden explosion as the hull was breached and the vacuum of space claimed the remains. My Susan was a shattered collection of glass shards and broken dreams. The trip back to K-Mart was deafeningly silent. The store was completely sold out of Partridge Family thermoses, so I had to settle for what remained on the shelves.

Anyone know if a 1972 vintage Holly Hobby thermos is worth anything?

WOODLAND ELEMENTARY SCHOOL: PLAYGROUND CONFIDENTIAL

Woodland Elementary School came with its own proving ground, although outsiders often wrote it off as nothing more than a simple PLAYground. Those of us who ran through that unforgiving and cruel jungle know better. The playground at Woodland was actually a bit schizophrenic. There were sections designated as safe for grades K-3, then other areas deemed suitable. for the more discerning 4th to 6th grade crowd. This 38th parallel was never actually marked with a physical line on the asphalt or anything, but the younger kids instinctively knew when they were getting perilously close to crossing over it. It was Stow's version of a prison shock collar, only without the explosive charges. The K-3 crowd had to content themselves with games like hopscotch, which was barely a game in the first place, and the dreaded small swings. The teeter-totters were also divided between amateur and professional grade, although the one "game" that became universal was the sudden jump from the lower position, allowing gravity to take care of the victim in the higher position.

One popular playground game evolved from the innocent version we all played in the school's so-called multipurpose room. For a while, it was the gym for indoor PE classes, then it morphed into the lunchroom for meals, then became a gym again until the artistic urge took over and it became the auditorium for school talent shows or outside performances or whatever. While it was still a gym, however, we played the game known as dodgeball. Dodge ball was the straightforward version—there's a ball, dodge it. There was a natural upper limit to how much pepper could be put on those odd rubber balls only sold to schools, apparently. Throw, dodge, retrieve, throw again, hit, leave. These were all graspable concepts to a 4th grader.

Somewhere along the way, dodgeball became fireball. Fireball was similar to dodgeball only in the sense that fast-pitch baseball was similar to slow-pitch softball. Fireball was serious business, played by serious people. I remember one guy at Kimpton Middle School who could pick off any target of his choosing from across the entire gym floor. You could try to catch the ball, you could try to get out of the way, you could try to feign injury and leave, but Mark was eventually going to nail you with that fireball. Death by round rubber was in the cards. Once Mark got through picking off most of the opposing team, one unfortunate survivor who spent the entire game hiding behind others would be the last one standing. The PE teacher would declare a free fire zone, meaning there were no more lines standing between competitors. Mark would stalk his prey for a few minutes, then deliver a crushing blow from three feet away. I think we ended up giving Mark both ears and the tail one time.

There was another game that was actually banned by the principal during my time at Woodland. Many of us can still remember the last words we heard before our collective lights went out: "Red Rover, Red Rover, let Mikey come over!". Red Rover was definitely a team sport, with two lines of players facing each other from a distance. The idea was to link arms and form an impenetrable human chain. A captain would select a challenger from the other side and lead his or her team in the taunting chant "Red Rover, Red Rover, let (insert name here) come over!". With that simple request, Inserted Name would try to break through the chain by any means necessary. If he or she was successful, a player would be sent back to the other side. If he or she could not break through, they became the newest link in that chain. This process of brute force elimination could stretch on for a while, I remember.

The Red Rover rot set in after more than a few Insert Names Here came on over as requested and failed miserably. Either they got clotheslined by the strongest links, or they inadvertently took out a few links of their own during an open-field tackle situation. The Red Rover victim-to-champion ratio became far too lopsided for the principal's liking, so he sent out a general bulletin that our Red Rover playing days were over. I remember a few people were sorely disappointed that their best head-butting days were now behind them, but it was a banner day for Insert Names Here everywhere.

One afternoon at Woodland, I watched two of our janitors drill a hole in the playground blacktop. They installed a tall aluminum pole and anchored it into the ground with cement. One of the janitors attached a long string to a hook at the very top of the pole, then attached what appeared to be a volleyball to the other end of the string. Without much fanfare, the internationally ignored sport of tetherball had come to Stow. None of us knew exactly how the game was supposed to be played, but eventually the PE teacher did take us outside and explained the basic rules of tetherball. At long last, here was a game that made as little sense as possible and we actually stood in line waiting to play it. The best part was that helpless feeling at the very end as you watched your opponent wrap that ball around the pole at lightning speed.

One version of tetherball started out as a straight punch service, with the goal being to get past the other player and wrap the entire cord around the pole in a certain direction. This could be done through brute force or finesse, depending on the player's anger management skills. The other version called for the ball to swing slowly around the pole a few times in one player's direction, and then players could pounce on the ball at will. This was the version of tetherball that confused me the most. What other game on Earth started with one team watching helplessly as the other team loaded most of the bases? That three-turn advantage was devilishly hard to overcome, yet we would dutifully watch the ball wind around the pole like lemmings until that third spin. Tetherball was clearly a game sold to school administrators, not to the kids.

One "game" unique to Woodland was not really a game at all, but more of a dare. The back of the school's designated playground extended into a small woods. To keep students from wandering too far into those woods, rings were painted on several trees to serve as borders. The woods on one side of those border trees looked pretty much like the woods on the other side, but rules were rules. We were NOT to travel beyond those ringed trees, ever ever ever. Of course, there was no faster way to get some of us to disobey a school rule than by telling us not to do it.

By the time I was in 5th grade, the mythology of the Land Beyond The Painted Trees had become huge. There were stories of evil men who kidnapped trespassing children, who were of course never seen again. That was a good one for me—I would sometimes even stand guard near the ringed trees and look for anyone even a little suspicious. There were also tales of bears or coyote packs hiding in those woods, just waiting for free kids' meals. Perhaps the best deterrents were all of those apocryphal stories about the punishment that awaited anyone who was caught behind those trees. In the unspoken Woodland criminal codes, crossing over into the Forbidden Zone during school hours was at the top of the list. I knew a few people who paid dearly for that brief taste of life outside the compound. I found out later, however, that there was a nice little trail that ran through those woods, and it ended at one of the least scary places in Stow—the Stow-Kent Shopping Center. The school system spent years scaring us away from Kresge's department store and the A&P.

Have The Sirens Stopped Screaming, Clarice? The Stow 4th of July Parade, Sponsored By Beltone

The Victorians essentially perfected the Christmas holiday season, and the Puritans put a clear thumbprint on the celebration we now call Thanksgiving. However, the city of Stow OWNED the 4th of July; the competition was and still is for second place. Other cities may think they can assemble an acceptable bevy of Shriner midget cars, high school bands, beauty queens, and themed floats, but when I was a child in the early 1970s, the Stow, Ohio Fourth of July parade operated on a completely different plane of existence. Route 59 through town became the epicenter of a 3-hour tribute to the civic duty gods.

The parade started assembling at the Stow-Kent Shopping Center, which was really the only location on that end of the street capable of supporting so many parade entrants. The parade route was one street running east to west, terminating at a review stand several miles away in the so-called downtown section of Stow. The mayor and other dignitaries would congregate at that review stand, but most of us regular folk would find a spot along Kent Road, pull out an old-school lawn chair, and wait for clear signs of an impending parade. We usually didn't have to wait long. A few police officers on motorcycles would clear the stragglers off the street just before the largest peacetime armada of emergency vehicles ever assembled started the festivities.

In the annals of historically bad ideas, one immediately springs to mind: Assembling a collection of fire trucks and ambulances from a three-county area and having them drive single-file down the same stretch of densely populated highway. The CONCEPT of seeing a fleet of shiny fire trucks driving down our street sounded promising indeed to a 6-year-old. However, the execution was a completely different story. As part of the parade ritual, all of these emergency vehicles decided to turn on their lights and sirens at the same time and for the same duration, which is to say, forever. The cumulative effect of all of those outside voices was mind-numbing deafness, which lingered for the rest of the now-silent parade. To add audio insult to sonic injury, some of those fire engines also blew their diesel horns, which entered our bodies at the ear canal and exited out of places we forgot we had.

After the Beltone-sponsored parade of emergency vehicles passed by, life along the sidelines got a little easier. The American Field Service volunteers would walk up and down the parade route, hawking very small American flags that we would dutifully wave at the parade participants. For us kids, this was all leading up to the most important part of the parade: the candy toss. This was no small thing. Someone on a passing float would toss a handful of candy in our direction and a sugar-fueled feeding frenzy would begin. Every once in a while, an errant pitch would send the bulk of the candy in one direction and one direction only. Mine. Before I could pack up all of that Bubble Yum or Tootsie Roll booty, however, my mom would remind me of my Gallant tendencies and I'd end up redistributing it to the less fortunate. Darn the less fortunate.

One group that both scared and excited me was the Shriners, or as I thought of them, the old guys with the funny hats. At one point, their stunt vehicles of choice were Honda mini-bikes, which they would ride in intricate formations at different points along the route. Before going into their routine, however, a few of the flying monkey men would zip across the sidelines to make sure no groundlings were in the path of the mini-bikes. That little safety maneuver scared me to death, since I was often too busy picking up stray candy to notice a Shriner barreling down on top of me with 50 ccs of raw power behind him. The Shriners later switched to those miniature clown cars, which seemed to ratchet back the drama of non-athletic competition, in my younger opinion. You could only do so much damage in a clown car, and if these men thought riding mini-bikes designed for 8-year-olds made them look like dorks on parade, the cars were not exactly babe wagons, either.

What happened next could only be described as an object lesson in terminal whiteness. The area high school bands would all march down the parade route in a stupefyingly predictable order: Majorettes, banner, drum major, band, band directors. Majorettes, banner, drum major, band, band directors. The upper funk limit for most of these bands was Stevie Wonder's "Sir Duke". Bands from Tallmadge, Hudson, Cuyahoga Falls, Kent, and most notably, Stow, would take turns performing these squeaky tight Marvin the Martian arrangements of traditional march music and fight songs. Stow's fight song was the same as Ohio State's: "Across the Field" (alternative lyrics not included). Precision was the underlying theme, and for the most part, we appreciated the homage to discipline and order. We were still Midwesterners, after all.

But nothing, NOTHING, prepared us for the volunteer drum corps from Akron. They wore purple and black uniforms, and clearly brought the funk from the county seat. No clarinets, no flutes, no saxophones; just trumpets and a boatload of drums. These guys didn't march in hyper-straight formations; they didn't really "march" at all. They eased on down the road with a solid BOOM-CHAKA-LAKA, BOOM-CHAKA-LAKA backbeat driving them the whole way. As a young, frightened Caucasian, I had read the forbidden texts concerning funk, but during the Stow 4th of July parade, I actually had a chance to experience it in person. I liked it. I really liked it.

One of the more interesting, and one would think least innocent bystander-friendly, participants in the parade were the stunt shooters from Akron. At regular intervals along the route, a volunteer sitting in the back of an open-bed truck would hold out a balloon and shout "Fire!". At this point, the three trick shooters walking behind the truck would whip out their six-shooters and shoot the balloon dead. These people were lightning-fast and extremely accurate, two qualities I admired in stunt shooters walking down a crowded street with live ammunition. I found out later that they only shot wax bullets, which would disintegrate on contact with the balloon. The version inside my eight-year-old mind was much better.

The floats were almost always from the "Red, White and Blaine" school of civic pride, and it was always interesting to see someone I knew from school or church strapped to one, but I noticed that some of my friends couldn't handle the pressures of sudden float fame. They would Bogart the candy, for one thing. After all, we had been through from Kindergarten to July 3rd of that year, the least a buddy on a Stow Lions Club float could do was hook a brother up with that sweet, sweet Tootsie Roll action. Ingrates.

Perhaps nothing explains the Stowbilly psyche better than the ignoble end of all 4th of July parades. The parade participants who routinely gathered the most applause and adulation from the crowd weren't the high school bands, the gleaming and historical emergency vehicles, or the local civic leaders. We saved our loudest cheers for the rows of street cleaners with their cheerfully waving drivers, who closed out the parade in style. Well, except for those of us who watched our last shot at Bazooka Joe and Dum Dums get swept away forever.

WORKMAN HIGH SCHOOL:
Nothing a Ramp and Skinner Can't Handle

Practically every major building within the city limits of Stow served some other purpose at some other time in history. The building I knew as Workman High School, the one that serviced primarily 9th and 10th grade students, was at one time Stow High School, the only 9th-12th grade game in town. As Stow's population grew, the original building became hopelessly outgunned by the incoming student bodies. As many of us Stowbillies fondly remember, the city's solution to the problem was to find the best and the brightest architects it could afford, and these skilled men would come up with a solid plan to double the capacity of Stow High School. This scheme would have worked, too, if it hadn't been for those meddling measurements. The new addition was precisely one half-floor higher than the original building. Sorry about that, chief. Missed it by *that* much.

The marriage between old and new sections of Workman was finally achieved with a long, sloping ramp down the middle of a connecting hallway. Few of us missed any opportunity to slide or roll something down that ramp back in the day. The new section also had an elevator, although permission to use said elevator was limited to handicapped students or those who were temporarily out of commission. The rest of us had to choreograph an intricate ballet involving ramps, stairwells, hallways and more hallways. Workman's floor plan was dictated by the educational philosophy championed by Dr. Benjamin Skinner, a leading specialist in draconian teaching methods at the time. Dr. Skinner believed all a student really needed to learn was a desk and a teacher. Like rats in a maze, each student would eventually figure out the optimum way to travel from classroom to classroom. The reward for all of this behavioral conditioning was a quality education with minimal distractions. I would have preferred a lump of cheese myself.

The original part of Workman still featured steam-fed radiators for heat and open windows for non-heat. There was no air conditioning for the comfort of the rat students or their rat instructors. Dr. Skinner would have loved what they did with the place. During the colder months, the steam heat would flow through the cold metal pipes, causing them to expand and contract. This expansion and contraction triggered a series of loud bangs that could be heard throughout the building. It became our two minute warning that heat was finally on the way, one hallway at a time. The new part of Workman also had steam heat, but the architects were

clever enough to hide the pipes under more modern covers. We could actually twist knobs that looked like they would have some effect on something. They didn't. Welcome to Ramp World.

One hallway in the original section led to the typing room, where many of us learned how to type on manual typewriters. The instructor would put on a record, and a man who sounded suspiciously like the narrator of every school filmstrip ever would call out letters to type. As we tapped our way through the "A...S...D...F...J...K...L...Sem" assignment over and over again, we had plenty of time to think of the things we'd rather be doing, like not typing endless lines of asdfjkl;. I always thought a sentence like "All work and no play makes Jack a dull boy." would be more interesting, just to see the look on the janitor's face when he emptied out trashcans from The Shining.

Our typing teacher at Workman did find ways to break up the homerow monotony, especially on Friday mornings. She allowed students to bring in their own albums while the rest of us sawed away at assignments printed in a workbook. I'm not sure if she was aware of the artistic leanings of the modern music scene at the time, but she wanted to be hip to the jive and we weren't about to stop her. Because we were so isolated from the rest of the building, volume was not an issue. So those of us who took certain typing courses under a certain typing/ English teacher during the early 80s all learned to type while listening to AC/DC's heavy metal album "Back in Black". To this day, I can still hear the clacking of typewriter keys timed to the beat of the title song or "You Shook Me All Night Long".

The library at Workman was not especially spacious, but it was clearly a library, not a Kimptonian instructional resource center. The head librarian was one of those school employees you just knew had been there since brick one of construction. We called her the Mole Lady behind her back, but as deaf as she was, I'm sure we could have bypassed the pretense altogether. The standard procedure for checking out a book from the Workman library was to fill out a card with the student's name and hand it over to the librarian or her assistant for date stamping. This system should have worked well, except for the inevitable Stowbilly factor. A number of students would put a much different name on the card, from Haywood Jablome to Ben Dover. This would usually amount to a whole lot of nothing, since the books would be returned on time anyway and the name used on the card didn't really matter to the circulation assistant.

However, this flaw in the system did backfire spectacularly one day during study hall in the cafeteria. The Mole Lady herself came down from the library, which by Workman hallway standards probably took most of the morning, then approached one of the study hall monitors. She held a book card in one trembling hand, and in her inimitable craggy voice said "Attention, students, attention. We have an overdue book situation. Would Mr. JOHN please report to the library? Mr...ELTON... John?". We were all stunned. We didn't know whether to laugh or cry. She was completely sincere, and completely unaware that Elton John was a British singer-songwriter who had graduated years ago. Finally, someone shouted from the back of the room: "Elton's not here today, ma'am. He's on tour with Peter Frampton." Without missing a beat, the Mole Lady said "Well, would you please tell Mr.

John to see me in the library when he gets back? It's very important that I speak with him." And then she was gone.

The original section of Workman was clearly built during a different time than my own. There were secrets around every corner, and most of them were inspired by the Red Menace scare of the 1950s. The small gym in the basement, which my predecessors often used as a makeshift dance hall during lunch, also served as an official atomic bomb shelter. A storage room connected to the gym still contained the remnants of emergency food supplies from the 1950s. There was also a tunnel which led from that storage room to the basement of the City Hall building. The City Hall building also had the iconic Civil Defense Shelter signs from the blissful "Duck and Cover" days. Considering the size of the student population at Workman and the capacity of the underground gym and bunker, there may have been a discussion or two in the day about who would get to enjoy the emergency rations and who would be toast during an actual atomic event.

The newer section of Workman housed many of the science classrooms, which meant access to Bunsen burners and a few serious chemicals. One of my favorite biology teachers was also an amateur bodybuilder, so his class lectures would often include the phrase "getting huge", followed by a Schwarzenegger-inspired pose or two. He would also perform experiments which were clearly not sanctioned by the school, but were usually fun to watch. One experiment involved pouring two liquid compounds together in a very tall glass cylinder. Nothing happened for a few minutes, but he explained that some chemicals generate significant heat when combined and we should just keep watching. A minute later, a steaming hot foam rose from the top of the cylinder, spilled over the side and flowed over the desk. The foam continued to slide along the floor and then out the classroom door.

What we may have called an exothermic reaction on the test soon became a smoldering pile of goo in the hallway.

The restrooms at Workman varied in overall quality and usability. The showers in the locker rooms were legendarily bad, followed closely by the student restrooms by the north entrance. In an effort to thwart smokers, the doors to each stall had been removed, which was not as much of a deal breaker on the boys' side as it was for the girls' side. Our assistant principal would periodically receive reports of illicit smoking in the girls room and throw a bucket of water through the front entrance. His actual smoker to poor girl just trying to brush her hair before class ratio was pretty abysmal, however. Other restrooms were much better, and the ones in the teachers' lounges were the best of all. This may explain why so many teachers went into apoplectic fits whenever a student wandered into the lounge by mistake. They were zealously protecting their pristine bathroom stalls, replete with working doors and abundant ashtrays.

They say all barely adequate but legally sufficient things must pass, and the Workman building was no exception. After the new 9th through 12th grade Stow-Munroe Falls High School became operational during the late 80s, the Workman building was generally abandoned. It would eventually be torn down, and the land would be converted for retail use. Many young Stowites would never guess an entire high school once stood on the property where Marc's is today. Many older Stowbillies, however, still remember running laps around the field behind the building, walking down to the public library after school, or hanging out at Eddie's bike shop or the Lawson's parking lot. The Workman building (and its surprisingly good cafeteria) may be gone, but many of us will miss that old Skinner box and its promise of better cheese to come.

Silence of the Chipped Chopped Hams

Growing up in Stow meant developing a taste for cheap cold cuts, especially those containing the word "loaf." Grocery stores like Acme Click and Reinker's had deli departments with the usual selections of ham, roast beef and turkey, but it rarely stopped there. Those meats lived on the right side of the sliced meat tracks, but were usually too expensive for our school lunch bags or Dad's lunchbox. The working class cold cuts lived on the poorly lit side of the deli case. Their names were Dutch loaf, ham loaf, pickle loaf and the dreaded olive loaf. Many of us still remember going to school with little brown bags filled with a Dutch loaf sandwich on white bread, a postage stamp sized bag of corn chips and an apple. My mother would occasionally spread a thin layer of margarine across the bread before applying the mayonnaise, apparently in an effort to keep the bread from becoming soggy. It really only converted an already questionable sandwich into a not-quite-butter flavored questionable sandwich.

The loaf meats became a staple in many Stowbilly households, but the *capo de capo* of inexpensive lunch meats had to be a processed ham loaf chipped off the slicer as thinly as possible. This was, of course, chipped chopped ham (or chip chop, if you lived at my house). Chipped chopped ham was noticeably less expensive than its more accomplished honey or smoked ham brethren. This amalgamation, formed and pressed from different ham sources, was then placed on a special slicer capable of making exceptionally thin cuts while the loaf was slammed repeatedly against the blade. The result was a remarkably flavorful cold cut which was more art than science. A huge mound of chipped chopped ham from Isaly's or Click would only set the family back a dollar or so, and it was awesome when pan fried with barbecue sauce or ketchup. Fresh white bread was the only logical choice for a sandwich accompaniment in our household.

For the younger Stowbilly on the move, interested in looking cool at any cost, a toothpick was an essential tool, and the flavor of the day was cinnamon; the hotter, the better. Several drugstores sold an array of flavored oils, from spearmint to citrus to cotton candy. By far the most popular flavor among those in the know was cinnamon. The thing to do was buy a box of wooden toothpicks and a bottle of cinnamon oil, then soak a supply of toothpicks in the cinnamon oil bottle for at least 24 hours—longer if you were in sadomasochism or self-immolation. These hot toothpicks could be brought to school legally, since they were clearly not chewing or bubble gum. Chewing on an especially pickled cinnamon toothpick became a rite of passage for some of us.

The other cinnamon-based product many of us carried to school were miniature jawbreakers known as Atomic Fireballs. As with the chipped chopped ham, Isaly's became a popular source for these individually wrapped balls of fire. A kid could buy a substantial amount of Atomic Fireballs for a quarter at Isaly's, then resell them at a profit during regular school hours. They became a form of sugar-laden currency, and any 6th grade boy packing some serious Atomic Fireball heat became the man other men wanted to be, and all the women wanted to be with. No, seriously. I mean it.

Pizza was another hot commodity in Stow, and there were some legendary rivalries between suppliers. Altieri's had the hometown advantage, since just about everyone in town knew anyone who had ever owned the place. Parasson's had the field advantage, since it was situated on the same street as the original high school. Bella Vista had it for authenticity, since very few people outside of Italy itself could have possibly been as Italian as the brothers who operated it. My personal favorite, however, was Angelina's, which had no tactical advantage whatsoever. It was situated in a wedge between two streets, and patrons had to climb several concrete steps to even reach the front door. Angelina's pizza oven ran so hot that it routinely burned the toppings to a pleasant crisp. This was a plus in my book.

Parasson's was a memorable dining venue all by itself. Early in its history, the building was used as an inn and also a restaurant that introduced the idea of an all-inclusive smorgasbord to our humble little burg (for non-Midwesterners, an all-inclusive smorgasbord is another term for an all-you-can eat buffet). When it became an Italian restaurant, the owners took advantage of the floor plan and converted each room into themed dining areas: English Tudor, Italian, garden greenhouse and so on. Regulars would know to ask the hostess for a specific room, but those outside the loop would usually end up in the glass-enclosed greenhouse room in the middle of August. Nothing on the menu was better than the dark rumor that passed from generation to generation, however. The claim was that the building also served as a funeral home before it became a family-friendly Italian restaurant. The word on the street was that several former restaurant employees had been dispatched to the basement for supplies and discovered: A) A secret room used for embalming bodies. B) The remains of an oven used for cremations. or C) An elevator used to transport caskets to the viewing rooms above.

The other food-related rivalry that many Stowbillies experienced first-hand involved ice cream and ice cream novelties. Isaly's built its reputation on the quality of its hard-packed ice cream, which would be dipped out of a coffin freezer and pressed into a sugar cone or one of those styrofoamesque cones with an internal support structure Frank Lloyd Wright would have admired. For those who preferred their ice cream with some chew and moral heft, Isaly's was clearly the way to go. Isaly's ran a small short-order diner in the back area, and milkshakes or sundaes made from one of 20-plus flavors were very popular.

Close to Isaly's was another ice cream joint that was so nice they named it at least twice. When I was very young, during the early 70s, the place was called PDQ, short for Pretty Darn Quick. I wouldn't know; I just sat in the car. I remember there was an eggnog-flavored powdered milk additive also called PDQ, so I would order an eggnog milkshake from PDQ. PDQ changed hands and became Stow Cone. Stow Cone kept up many of the traditions established by PDQ, and was especially popular after school sporting events. The back of the parking lot also happened to be the top of an impressive natural gorge, however, so making that left turn out of the drive-through lane was always a good decision.

Although not technically within the city limits, for many of us, the final word on all things ice cream was found at a frozen custard stand called Stoddard's. Stoddard's did not serve that simple peasant dish known as ice cream. No, it served frozen custard—the dairy product our mothers warned us about. Frozen custard had a much higher percentage of butterfat than regular ice cream, and the machines' agitators turned twice as slowly, which meant far less air in the final product. Quite fairly, frozen custard stands have been described as the places where God gets His ice cream. Stoddard's was definitely one of our local houses of worship. A single scoop of Stoddard's frozen custard cost 25 cents at one point, but woe unto the child who had to stop short for traffic and watch his beloved custard fall off the cone and onto the ground.

Because frozen custard was a labor-intensive process and they only owned three machines, Stoddard's only produced three flavors at a time: Vanilla, Chocolate and the Flavor of the Day. The vanilla was awesome, the chocolate was powerfully good, but the flavor of the day was always a crap shoot. Some days it would be something amazingly good, like banana or strawberry or blueberry, while other days it would be something not so tempting, like pineapple or butterscotch or mint chocolate chip. A small sign near the roadside announced the flavor of the day, and I would adjust my stride according to the selection. If it was blueberry, dead sprint. If it was pineapple, slow crawl. If it was mint chocolate chip, my least favorite at the time, tactical retreat. Stoddard's was a ritual for those of us who attended the Apostolic Pentecostal church 200 yards away, as well as for those who happened to live in a house 210 yards away.

There were a lot of other foodstuffs from that time many of us Stowbillies still crave to this day. Lawson's was a convenience store chain with locations spaced out about every hundred yards or so. One of its most popular products was a French onion dip so good that people simply dropped every extraneous word to describe it. It was simply Lawson's Chip Dip. Nothing tasted better on a wavy potato chip or a Doritos tortilla chip (or for that matter, cardboard), than Lawson's Chip Dip. When Lawson's franchises began to disappear from the landscape, the new convenience store chains made every effort to keep that same French Onion dip stocked on their shelves.

My mother used to make a comfort food she called tuna macaroni salad, and one ingredient became so popular that it was often used in place of the term "salad dressing" in church cookbooks. Cooks did not add two cups of salad dressing to anything; they added Spin Blend. Spin Blend was a zippy little number with a distinctive green lid and attitude to burn. The official list of ingredients only mentioned lemon juice and vinegar, but we all knew in our Stowbilly hearts that here there be horseradish. Spin Blend turned an ordinary cold pasta salad into an explosion of Pennsylvania Dutch-inspired madness. Spin Blend could even turn a Dutch loaf or chipped chopped ham sandwich into one of the best sandwiches any kid ever put in his lunch bag, even with that obscene swath of greasy margarine standing between the meat and the aptly-named Wonder bread.

There are many other favorite Stowbilly foods and beverages that did not get mentioned in this essay, but trust me they will get their day in the sun in future issues. I'm thinking about Wacky Packs, Sto-nut donuts, JoJo potato wedges, burgers at the Flagpole, and whatever pickled thing was in that jar on the counter at Eddie's. No journey would be complete without trips to the Red Barn, Rax, Around the Clock and Osman's Pies, either. Stay tuned. There's a lot more nostalgia where this came from.

LAKEVIEW HIGH SCHOOL:
Incidentally, No Lake and No View

Somewhere between Kimpton's wild 60s architectural excesses and Workman's staple-as-you-go utilitarianism was Lakeview High School, the final 2 in Stow's clearly improvised 2-2-2 higher education plan. When Workman ceased to be workable as Stow's sole 9-12th grade high school, Lakeview became the "new" high school, thoughtfully located a quarter of a mile away from the existing one. There are those who still recall the day when the first class scheduled to graduate from Lakeview made its historic trek from Workman to the Lakeview campus. As the school yearbook would document, these pioneers weren't about to let a construction fence get in the way of educational progress, no sir.

Some of us Workmanites first experienced Lakeview as members of the marching band. Those freshmen and sophomore students would get off the buses at Lakeview and assemble on the practice field while the rest of us rode an additional quarter of a mile to Workman. Following band practice, there would be a parade of young band members walking to the Workman campus, while others made their way up to Lakeview for drivers' education classes. That walk between Lakeview and Workman could either be a welcome break from the Skinner box or an object lesson on why others leave NE Ohio in droves during winter months. Since the class times did not always take into account the commute between campuses, most of us developed a walking pace somewhere between deliberate and alarmingly laser-focused.

Lakeview also featured a parking lot for both students and faculty, a situation which naturally cried out for a sense of law and order. The responsibilities of this position fell on one man and one man only, and that man had a name: One Bullet Barney, aka Rent-a-Cop.

Barney indeed took his job very seriously, even if the driving student population did not. Getting past the Rent-a-Cop was the first step in a multi-step plan to get to McDonald's and back during the lunch period. The final step was getting back on campus while Barney was distracted by other student drivers working on step one. Getting a citation from Barney usually carried about as much weight as getting an overdue book notice from the Mole Lady at Workman, but few Stowbillies wanted to stay on his bad side for very long. He had a long memory, and a few friends still on the force.

Although the parking lot situation could be troubling at times, it paled in comparison to the vandalism magnet we euphemistically called the courtyard. The courtyard's centralized location and restricted access seriously harshed its buzz as a functional space, but it still served a purpose for senior classes during the last weeks of school. The aforementioned McDonald's restaurant had one thing every senior class hoped to capture, but only a handful ever did. Once every few years, a clearly disgruntled maintenance staff would have to fish a large fiberglass horse out of the courtyard, the same statue usually found in front of the Golden Arches of Stow. Sometimes a few crudities would be "painted" with bleach on the vulnerable courtyard grass, while at other times very large items would be dismantled and reassembled in the courtyard's confined space. If it was large and missing within five miles of Stow (especially during late May), searching in Lakeview's courtyard would not have been a bad idea.

Much like Kimpton's bucket of french fries or Workman's revered peanut butter bars, Lakeview's cafeteria had one feature that kept the faithful coming back for more. The standard lunch was generally satisfying, but for only an additional quarter students could stand in line for what was promoted as a chocolate milkshake. In retrospect, the fact that the milkshake mix was provided by the spoilsports at the

USDA should have been a clue. It may not have been on a par with Friendly's or Stoddard's, but at least it was cold and creamy. Chocolaty, however, it was not. Nevertheless, many of us with two bits burning a hole in our pockets would dutifully stand in line all lunch period for a shot at natural dairy product goodness. The milkshake line also featured a few other snack items generally not found on the standard lunch menu, such as potato chips and candy bars. It was an alternative nation, a wink and a nod to nutritional mutiny in a lunchroom dedicated to the vagaries of the subsidized lunch program.

Lakeview during the early 80s was the site of a few other social experiments, like the ill-fated attempt to change the school's colors to pink and black and adopt a new mascot: The Stow High Good and Plentys. There were plenty of valid signatures on that petition, but unfortunately decades of maroon and gold tradition did not play in our favor. Another science project could be described as "one milk carton, one unused locker". After several months, the consensus among us scientists was that milk cartons were incredibly resilient, but things could only continue in one unfortunate direction. An unwashed gym shirt we named Fred Bread was also left in an unused locker for several months, but that experiment ended during a surprise locker inspection, which yielded a few illegal substances, some Playboy magazines and a green, fuzz-covered gym shirt. Fred Bread taught us a lot about living, about dying, and what it was to be a man. Actually, he taught us the value of a roll of quarters and a cup of laundry detergent.

One positive thing about the Lakeview campus was there was everything in a room and a room for everything. The building itself was almost a military-industrial complex in scope, with metal and wood shops, a massive gymnasium and locker rooms, band and choir rooms, business school rooms for IOE students, a darkroom for yearbook and newspaper photographers, not to mention offices for teachers and classrooms for everything from Latin to physics. The only catch was that students had five minutes at best to travel between all of those areas. Logistics rarely entered the equation whenever we were selecting our classes for the next semester. Anyone who signed up for Algebra II and choir, for example, would have to run from the last room of the top floor on the north side of the building to one of the last rooms on the bottom floor of the south side. The first bell served two purposes: the end of the class period, and the start of the daily 300 yard dash to the gym's locker room.

One class at Lakeview became very popular because of Ohio state law. A would-be driver under the age of 18 was required by law to present a certificate of completion from a recognized driver's ed school. Those who could afford the tuition fees had the option of attending what we liked to call a "crash course" on driving. Sear's offered a four day driver's ed course that satisfied at least the spirit of the law. Successful students would indeed receive a certificate of completion and could take their driving test in Cuyahoga Falls. However, there were many of us who enjoyed turning that kind of privileged positive into a Stowbilly negative. If a driver in the Stow area ever did something hazardous, like stopping short or failing to signal a turn, many of us would yell "Where did you learn to drive? SEARS?".

Meanwhile, the rest of us who were of driving age would sign up for the school-sponsored driver's ed course at Lakeview. This meant 18 weeks of classroom, simulator and real world training, but at least we wouldn't drive like those heathens with the Cracker Jack box certificates. The driver's ed instructor had exactly the demeanor you would expect from a social studies teacher shanghaied into teaching 16 years how to handle a 3,000 pound Deathmobile. He was fond of pointing out that he was a fervent bicyclist, so he was essentially giving us the means and ability to run him off the road later. We would watch the required "Blood Runs Red on the Highway" snuff films, spend time behind the wheel of a 1963 Studebaker in a driving simulator, then drive around town in a real car. The instructor did have a second brake installed on his side, however. At the end of the course, he doled out the certificates of completion, which he called "death certificates", and warned us all not to say anything approaching a thank you.

I'll end with one final memory of a teacher from Lakeview, a man who fought in Korea and enjoyed repeating his one good story about the place. It seems he was a hit with the local ladies because of his thick red hair, and they gave him a Korean nickname which he translated as "Number One Redhead". He taught history at Lakeview, although he was the kind of person I always thought should be *making* history somewhere else. I really enjoyed his class, and sometimes I would visit him during my 8th period study hall. He also owned a miniature golf course, so occasionally he would hand me a set of free passes to play a game or two. One day I walked into his empty classroom and found him watching TV. It wasn't a standard over-the-air channel, but an uncut cable movie channel. The cable television line ran on a pole right outside his classroom window, so he managed to splice some coaxial cable and tap into the signal. We watched Superman II for an entire class period, then I left to catch my bus. That's one of my lasting memories from my time spent at Lakeview High School, the building with no lake and no view, but still plenty of heart and soul.

The Revolution WILL Be Televised, at 2:30 In The Morning

Most Stowbilly children, especially teenagers, knew that the really good stuff didn't show up on TV until at least 11:30 on a Friday night. That's when Channel 8 in Cleveland handed over the reins to a weatherman and a broadcast engineer, AKA Hoolihan and Big Chuck. Hoolihan and Big Chuck's show was an amalgamation of schlocky horror movies, song parodies, Certain Ethnic jokes and sketch comedy clearly filmed on the cheap with someone else's equipment. It was pure camp, but we watched every last minute of it, all the way to the last segment where Hoolihan and Big Chuck, dressed in tacky animal print pajamas, would read jokes submitted by their loyal viewers. We needed to hear these jokes, because we would inevitably be retelling them at school on Monday morning. By the end of the broadcast, we would be too exhausted to move from the couch to the TV set, so we just let it run. We...just...let...it...run.

The end of Hoolihan and Big Chuck may have signaled the final gasp of local programming, but it was not the end of late night television as we knew it. Our sleep-deprived Midwestern minds could still be blown by the rock concerts featured on another channel. It may have been Don Kirschner's Rock Concert or The Midnight Special, like any of us could tell the difference at 1 in the morning. Whichever show it was, Cousin It and the Cousin It Band were usually getting down with their bad selves on a smoke-filled stage. All I remember is that they were scary to watch, but clearly devoted to their craft. They may have been the Allman Brothers, they may have been Blue Oyster Cult, they may have even been the Doobie Brothers or Foghat, but whatever it was, it was clearly a taste of music from the land of cool people. It's just too bad we weren't nearly awake enough to let sonic art wash over us.

For those of us whose parents did not believe in the beauty of cable television, another late night music show became our own version of MTV. NBC would show two hours of last year's hottest videos, but we didn't care. We got to see Adam Ant and Cyndi Lauper and Talking Heads and...well, those other guys with the hair. I think they had synthesizers, but don't quote me on that. While The Midnight Special and Rock Concert may have an abundance of soul, the late night video show on NBC had the promise of a Madonna-like product, sir. Life for a bleary-eyed Stowbilly boy became much better as soon as he learned a Go-Go or Bangle or Benatar would play a significant role in it. With the arrival of home VCRs, the late night music video show became one of the first things we learned to program on the timer.

Meanwhile, the comedy was still going strong on other channels, even if it took a turn to the left. If Saturday Night Live was the best American late night sketch comedy of its day, then SCTV was its hipper Canadian cousin. The cast of SCTV read like a Who's Who of comedy, from John Candy to Rick Moranis to Eugene Levy, with stops in-between for Martin Short, Andrea Martin, Joe Flaherty and Catherine O'Hara. SCTV, which stood for Second City Television, had the luxury of taping their segments over time, but they still maintained a sense of immediacy like Saturday Night Live. Characters like Doug and Bob McKenzie, horror show host Count Floyd and the Five Neat Guys became the stuff of legend. If another kid at school quoted the Farm Film Report ("he blowed up. He blowed up REAL good), then you knew he was hip to the same late night jive. It was one thing to stay up until the pajama jokes on Hoolihan and Big Chuck, but something else entirely if you stayed up until the end credits of SCTV. There were many Sunday mornings when devoted SCTVers would drag themselves to church or simply call in sick and sleep until noon.

There were other shows on network television that would have clearly been out of place at any other time. Some of us still remember the Uncle Floyd show, which was undoubtedly the strangest half-hour of the night. Uncle Floyd, as some of us discovered later, worked the same alternative comedy venues as Paul Reubens, aka Pee Wee Herman. His show could loosely be described as a talk show, although his guests were not generally known for their conversational skills, and his personal sidekick spent the entire show in a catatonic stupor. What made the Uncle Floyd show so entertaining was the fact that it just showed up at 2 or 3 in the morning, and was never actually listed in the local TV guide. This turned an otherwise *avant garde* comedy show into a "how did *this* show get a time slot?" subversive act of programming. Occasionally, the original Pee Wee Herman show, which should never be mistaken for the sanitized CBS version, would also show up on extremely late night television. Pee Wee's show often showcased the alternative, edgy, dark comedians and performers our parents should have warned us about. Yes, there really was a band called the Plasmatics. Yes, there really was a 2:30 in the morning. No, the Plasmatics and 2:30 in the morning shouldn't be in the same sentence when you're 12 years old and hopped up on Doritos and cheap soda.

Whenever extremely late night network television would fail us, there was always the audiovisual toss-up known as UHF. If the local UHF channels, like WUAB-43 or channel 61, hadn't already called it a night, they would usually show grade Z horror movies, like Attack of the Wasp Woman or The Flesh Eaters. I'm saying it now, this was a miscalculation of epic proportions. The Flesh Eaters' plot revolved around a group of very unpleasant people who survived a plane crash and were now trapped on a deserted island. Unbeknownst to them, but plenty beknownst to the 12 year old audience, they were also surrounded by alien flesh-eating bacteria. One unprotected step into the water and it would be a bubbly, fluorescent kind of death for someone. The only member of the cast I was hoping would go flesh eater-free was the plane's pilot, who reminded me of the guy who *should* have gotten the role of the Professor on Gilligan's Island. As it turned out, he did indeed escape the island, after figuring out a way to electrocute the little alien buggers in bulk. Creepy, creepy movie.

The other UHF channels held their own after-hours charm, including the public television station that decided to broadcast the next day's object lessons during the wee smalls. At three in the morning, even first grade math was a challenge. Another UHF channel, clearly from a distant location, showed fuzzy reruns of shows like Mr. Ed and The Munsters, two shows that are far too high concept at three in the morning. The freakiest opening credit of a television show ever has got to be the creepy marionette Lucille Ball dancing her way through "Here's Lucy!". Wrong, wrong, wrong.

One dirty little secret about UHF channels and the Stowbilly boys who watched them is about to be revealed. One UHF channel decided to dip its toe in the paid television market, which would include adult movies with adult content. Their plan was to scramble their signal at a certain time at night, then offer descrambling devices to paid subscribers. OUR plan, however, was to hope the engineer in charge of scrambling the signal would either shirk his duties or call in sick. The scrambled signal would be vaguely watchable, if a wavy, soundless negative of a picture could be defined as "watchable". We didn't care, as long as we could see flashes of wavy, negative breasts on an actress with black teeth. The station insisted on showing cheaply produced European sex comedies from the 1970s, most of which were based on familiar fairy tales. The experiment didn't last more than a few years, but during that time many of us received an incomplete education that would require years of careful descrambling.

Also by Michael Pollick

Michael Pollick's Proving Ground
Michael Pollick's Proving Ground
The Keepinnit Reels
The Keepinnit Reels 2: Acoustic Boogaloo